Upson Downes

Dottie Maley

AuthorHouse™
1663 Liberty Drive
Bloomington, IN 47403
www.authorhouse.com
Phone: 1-800-839-8640

Published by AuthorHouse 10/01/2014

ISBN: 978-1-4969-3530-4 (sc)
ISBN: 978-1-4969-3539-7 (hc)
ISBN: 978-1-4969-3540-3 (e)

Library of Congress Control Number: 2014915057

ACKNOWLEDGMENTS

I WISH TO EXPRESS MY DEEPEST gratitude to the two following people. Patty Baker, a former boss who over the years, has not only encouraged me to write but has given many hours of her time to correct my mistakes and make helpful suggestions. The other person is Jeannette Hill my sister who would leave me to my work, coming only to bring a cup of tea or suggest I get up and walk around. Without the two of them this book would still be simmering on the back burner.

Chapter 1

HORACE BINKBOTTOM PARKED HIS MAZDA Miata in a wide spot on the narrow road leading to the cove below, zipped his old hunting jacket up to his chin, crammed his fedora on his head and stepped out to take a look at the community of Upson Downes that lay below him. What he saw brought back childhood memories of when he was a kid and had hiked through this area before it was developed. It was the connecting rod he needed to make him realize he finally was home.

Back in the car he drove on down to the well manicured area and found the real estate office in an ivy covered club house. The lady who came forward to meet him introduced herself as Miss Reversnuck, the broker for Upson Downes Realty. She was a pleasant looking woman with smartly styled white hair that set off her deep blue eyes and dressed in black slacks, knee high boots and a diamond pattern black and white turtle neck sweater. Smiling, she said, "Good morning. How may I help you?"

Introducing himself, Horace said, "I've seen your ad in the paper for Upson "Downes and I'm here to check out the facility. I'm looking for a place in which to retire."

"Wonderful, I'd love to show you around. We take great pride in our community. Building has slowed for the winter but we do have one finished house available if you'd like to see it. It's located in a spot at the top of the only hill in here."

She showed him around the club house with its myriad of amenities including a favorite of his, a billiard room. When they were through she said, "I'd love to drive you up to see this house. I just have a feeling you might like it.

On the way Horace said, “I’m impressed at the way this place is laid out. The golf course winds like a thread through a needle between the houses and yet they themselves aren’t in full view of each other. Most unusual. I like that.”

The home Miss Reversnuck showed him was more than he ever dreamed he’d find, even to a hot tub area in a natural setting with small trees and flowering shrubs. There were floor to ceiling windows in almost every room and an incredible view of the golf course, lake and distant mountains. “I have to confess, I’m very impressed,” Horace told her. “My first inclination is to say yes, but I would like to think about it overnight,” and she agreed that was the proper way to go.

Driving back to town, Horace couldn’t get the house or Miss Reversnuck out of his mind. On an impulse he pulled into a parking lot and dialed her number on his cell. When she answered, he re-introduced himself and said, “Miss Reversnuck I’d like to buy that house I looked at. I can be in your office at one tomorrow afternoon if that works for you.”

She had seemed rather breathlessly excited and agreed to meet him but said she would love to have him come to lunch at the club house before their meeting. “Our small but excellent little restaurant is open for lunch and I’d love to have you see the wonderful osprey nest way up on a pole at one corner of the outside terrace. The osprey are fascinating to watch. Oh, and one other request. Please call me Amanda”

“I’d be delighted to join you Amanda,” Horace told her. “I’ll be in your office around noon, and thank you.”

When Horace arrived at Amanda’s office he was not only pleased but amazed to see her not in slacks, sweater and boots but in a pale lavender blouse with clouds of ruffles up the front and around the collar. Her deep purple pleated skirt with matching high heels showed off a pair of shapely legs. Then he noticed something he’d missed yesterday… a dusting of freckles across her nose. She invoked a picture of the two of them as children, scuffing barefoot down a dirt road hand in hand----he in overalls and plaid shirt, carrying her school books, and she in pigtails and blue and white polka-dot dress.

True to the yo-yo weather report the day was sunny and much warmer. On entering the small but beautifully appointed restaurant that overlooked the golf course, they opted to sit outside on the deck where they could watch the ospreys come and go with food for their babies. It was fun, but sitting at the table next to them were three men, obviously having the time of their lives under the influence of the beers they had consumed. Amanda introduced one of them to Horace as Norbert Balmer, a former fighter pilot now living at Upson Downes.

After they sat down Amanda explained quietly to Horace that Norbert was one of their biggest fund raisers, but also a very gregarious guy who sometimes got on peoples nerves with his loud tactics. As they were going over their menus they became aware that Norbert and his friends were becoming louder and louder with their laughter and conversation. Finally their lunch was served and as the waitress walked away one of the ospreys who apparently had also become annoyed at their noise, made a swooping dive and with dead ringer precision unloaded not only on their table but on them and their food. They jumped up in shock and indignation and ran into the club house.

On inspection, Amanda and Horace were amazed that not one drop had landed on their table or on them. While a waitress mopped up the residue, Amanda said with a giggle, "Welcome to Upson Downes and osprey country."

Through his laughter Horace said, "Amanda, you didn't tell me lunch came with entertainment. I've never seen anything like that,"

Amanda too laughed as she said "It comes with the territory, but tell me now, are you really serious about buying the house?"

"I am," said Horace. My mind is made up and I'm anxious to get settled. I even went so far as making enquiries about your establishment in town and you came up with a glowing report."

"Well, in that case, let's hurry on back to the office and get this deal on its way," Amanda said as she paid the bill.

Back at the office she had everything already laid out in order and after poring over papers including a last minute decision on his part to have a deck built on the front of the house, they reached an agreeable price at which time she told him that because of the iffy weather it would probably be February before he could settle in.

In the paper shuffle he noticed a ring she was wearing and commented, "Beautiful ring. Am I wrong to assume you will soon be a Mrs.?"

With a blush full of charm she said, "Yes, next fall."

She immediately changed the subject and said, "I see your business was as an investment counselor. Do you plan to continue with that?

"Heavens no, I'm going to relax and enjoy whatever is in that pot at the end of my rainbow, but I have to tell you, for the first time since arriving back home I really feel like I can get on with my retirement and leave the past behind me."

Smiling as she handed him a set of keys she said "I sincerely hope you'll enjoy living here. We do have a very diverse, colorful and fun collection of residents. Now surely you'll want to at least go look again at this house you just bought."

"It would be nice if moving in could be sooner, but I think I'd rather have the extra work done before taking that step, and yes, I'll go up to the house now. You're welcome to come along if you like."

He was not only surprised but pleased when she said "I'd love to come along."

Horace tucked Amanda into his Miata and once underway mentioned that not only had he been born here, but as a kid he'd climbed and skied a lot of these mountains. I've lived on the East Coast for so long I wasn't aware of this development. It must be a big asset to the area."

With a laugh she said, "At first, we weren't welcome, but now the locals look on us as a bit of a Midas touch. Economically we've helped, and a lot of the residents also do volunteer work in town. It's been a big step toward our acceptance."

When Horace unlocked the front door to the house they stepped into another world. Through the angled floor-to-ceiling windows with the breathtaking view of distant mountains and the lake beyond the cove, the late afternoon sun bathed the area in a surreal wash of golden color. They stood in momentary silence. Looking over at Amanda, Horace was suddenly very grateful he had her to share this moment with.

"Wow! This is going to be a hard act to follow. In this grandeur my furniture is going to look like a couple of matchsticks in the Taj Mahal," he said.

Their room to room tour through the house was interspersed by her silvery laughter and astute comment about colors and placement of furniture. Her suggestions were provocative and fun.

"Here's the place I love," said Horace as he opened a door. The room, glass enclosed on three sides had a long counter and sink on the other side. "I don't think I mentioned that I dabble in sculpting, and this is the perfect spot. Plenty of room where I don't have to keep cleaning up and putting stuff away all the time."

"You're also an artist?" asked Amanda.

"Heavens no. It's something I took up after my divorce to keep from going nuts. It got rid of a lot of my frustrations. The first thing I ever did was an alligator with a raised head, looking around for his next meal. I named it Tessie. It was good enough my instructor talked me into having it cast in bronze. I'm going to put it out by my front walk."

Completely satisfied and happy with his purchase, they headed back to the office and out of curiosity Horace asked, "Are you a local girl"?

"No, I'm from Illinois. My dad was in the Army and we moved a lot. My mom and I lived with him awhile in Europe and Japan. Those were wonderful experiences. When I was ready to go to college I went to U.C.L.A. where I majored in business."

"And that led you into real estate?"

"No, I married and had two children. My husband died six years ago, but I still had the two boys to care for and heard through a friend about this position and was hired. The lady I was replacing taught me a lot. I took some courses and here I am."

"Are the two boys still with you?"

"Oh no, they flew the coop a few years ago. Tom, the eldest is working as an assistant director for a Performing Arts Center in Seattle and Jerry has been among the busy bees down in Silicone Valley designing soft ware."

With a laugh Horace said, "You actually had a Tom and Jerry combo? That must have been fun."

"Actually it was, and believe it or not it was their favorite cartoon. By then the cartoons were all re-runs, but we bought a couple of sets of the old ones and the kids loved them. And you, you mentioned that you had been born here. Do you still have family around?"

"Oh yes. My mother still lives here. My dad died several years ago and my mom and I get along okay, but our relationship is best suited to neither of us having a real need to be involved in each other's lives. That way we get along. We still see each other, usually socially, but that's okay. It works for both of us. She will be delirious I bought a house. I know she was scared to death I might want to move into her big old house with her."

By now they were sitting in the parking lot at the clubhouse. Horace went around to help her out of the car and taking her hand he thanked her for her time as he said, "I know you'll keep me posted on all fronts of progress and thanks for going with me. I'd love to have you in to see the house again once I've moved in."

"You can count on it," she said.

Chapter 2

THE NEXT FEW WEEKS WHILE waiting for the house to be done and his furniture to arrive, were a restless time, especially being cooped up in the small apartment he'd rented. Aside from the spate of holiday parties, Christmas dinner with his Mother and a few hunting forays he felt there was really nothing he could accomplish except keep an eye on the improvements he was having done at the house. The big day finally arrived and as exciting as it started out, once the delivery van finally pulled away and he stood alone surrounded by huge boxes and crates, he had the distinct feeling of having been dumped on. "Surely all this 'stuff' doesn't belong to me," he kept saying. One bright spot had arrived in the form of a large flower bowl of African violets, a housewarming gift from Amanda. In his grumpy mood, he felt that the least she could have done was to bring it herself. However, his bronze alligator had been in the first crate opened and placing it among the bushes along the front walk had done wonders for his spirits.

Later that afternoon, the ringing of the door bell startled him. He was sure it was his mother, and at this point she was the last person in the world he wanted to see.

Yanking open the door with annoyance, he found himself looking down at a bantam sized woman with the brightest blue eyes he'd ever seen. Under her heavy unbuttoned winter coat she was clad in faded rolled up denims, pale pink sneakers, and a vivid pink shirt with the word Grandma, embroidered on it in several different languages. On her arm she toted a basket. On her head of white curly hair was a bright red baseball cap with the proclamation, Grandmas are Moms with lots of frosting.

Grinning up at him she said, "Hi there, we're your neighbors from down the hill. I'm Dotson and this long drink of water is my husband Ford. Last name's Pickup"

Behind her stood an angular man who towered a foot above her head. Stained heavy turtle neck sweater that looked like it had at one time been a cleaning rag was in contrast to what looked like new cargo pants. Heavy socks covered his feet which were tucked into Birkenstock sandals. His tanned and pleasant face puckered up in a smile as he stepped forward to shake Horace's hand.

"Excuse my appearance. I was cleaning out the garage when I heard a voice from on high proclaimin' we were fixin' to call on our new neighbor. As you can see, my CEO didn't give me much time to change clothes.

"On the contrary, I'm grateful you even thought of coming out in this weather. Aren't you cold in those shorts?"

"Nah, the cold doesn't bother me, I love it."

"For heaven's sake, quit your chit chat and tell the gentleman why we're here," his wife snapped.

Ford, with a shake of his head as he gestured toward her said, "She's the only woman I know who has power surges instead of hot flashes. Anyway, the missus figured you wouldn't have thought about doing any food shopping yet, so she fixed up some goodies to tide you over."

Overwhelmed by their thoughtfulness, Horace introduced himself and invited them in.

"Sure thing," Ford said, "but tell me, is that alligator out front a relative of yours?"

"Only a distant one---on my mother's side," Horace replied. As they wound their way to the kitchen he asked "Say, if I can find the makings, could I interest you folks in a drink?"

"No thank you," Dotson said. We're not here to take up your time".

Ford, looking like a wounded moose said, "It's not polite to turn down hospitality like that."

"Don't pay any mind to him, Dotson said. He'd trade his mother in for a beer."

Opening the bag they had brought he removed the lid of a still warm casserole, took a deep whiff and exclaimed, "Oh man, beef stew with lots of beef and vegetables. One of my favorites. Please, won't you pull up a box and sit down."

Ford said, "No, no. Tell you what. As the wife said, it looks like you have several days work ahead of you, so we'll be going now. We just wanted to welcome you home, and if you ever need help with anything, give a holler."

"I'm ever so grateful, and I'd love to have you back once I'm settled," he told them.

Scooting off a box she'd been sitting on Dotson said, "Well---- hope you like my cooking. If it doesn't agree with you give a hoot and we'll call the Rotor Rooter boys".

Holding the door open as he motioned her out, Ford said, "Wrong end dear."

Chapter 3

AFTER WHAT HAD SEEMED LIKE an eternity, Horace, with a sigh of relief, slumped on a sofa and surveyed his surroundings."Not too bad for an old bachelor," he muttered. Knowing that his mother was awaiting an invitation to survey the premises with a magnifying glass, he asked Amanda if she would come by and check everything out in case he'd made some gross error in furniture placement or color coordination.

She had graciously agreed and as it had the day they had first gone through the house together, the late afternoon sun lit up the premises in dramatic colors. Now with the furniture and carpets in place the house, in spite of its openness, took on an intimate look. Her four-star rating, put his mind at ease. Her only suggestion was that it would be smart to invite his mother at this same time of day.

He followed her suggestion and two day later, his mother sailed into the room as though on a slum tour. He watched with amusement when her expression, clearly meant to convey she was expecting a disaster area, turned to amazement.

"Horace, I don't believe what I'm seeing. This is fabulous. Surely you had help. I had no idea you possessed such a keen color sense, and that you had such beautiful furnishings. The oriental rugs and Tiffany lamps blend perfectly with the modern architecture. Are you sure you didn't have professional help?"

"In a way, yes I did. You and my ex-wife were excellent teachers."

He wasn't sure whether this tender exchange had anything to do with what happened next, but she suddenly took a keen interest in some of his small sculptures that were scattered about. "You know, I just can't get over the fact that you took up sculpting and can create such beautiful shapes. This one is so graceful. I realize it is abstract, but does it have a name that denotes what it represents?"

Aware at the moment of his mother's vulnerability he said in all seriousness. "That one is called Lust."

She almost dropped it as she reddened. "Don't do that to me," she admonished, "Your father did that all the time and I hated it."

"Sorry Mother. Sometimes you're such an easy target I can't resist. Well, now that my digs have passed muster, you'll have to bring your bridge buddies up for a game and a dip in the hot tub."

Blanching slightly she said, "You'd never get any of those ladies near that thing. I suppose you use it."

"Oh yes, but hey, get a glass of sherry into some of those gals and who knows what might happen."

"In the first place, none of them would ever get past that beast out by your front walk."

"Oh Tessie? She was one of my first sculptures, but seriously, please, give some thought to my invitation. It could be fun"

Rising to leave she said, "I'll call you." At the door she did something so uncharacteristic he knew he would always remember it. Standing on tiptoe, she gave him a kiss on the cheek "I'm glad you've come home son."

Under the glow of that episode he went off to meet the Pickups at the Homeowner's Association Meeting. Much to his surprise they had stopped by to tell him of the meeting. "You won't get bored. There are always some people on the warpath. No matter what comes up, they're against it," Ford told him.

"Yeah," Dotson added. "Sometimes some of those people are a real pain in the ---you know what."

It sounded to Horace like a full-blown shooting match and the type of thing he had hoped to avoid but decided that since he was now a home owner he'd best be aware of what was going on in his community supposedly on his behalf.

Ford hadn't been wrong. The Homeowners Meeting was fraught with fireworks but once the uncomfortable baptism into the font of bickering was over, the ensuing activities made him glad he had come. The Pickups introduced him to several other neighbors and at one point in the evening Dotson caught up with him to inquire how he was doing.

"Believe it or not, I've been invited to play bridge Friday night with Judge and Mrs. Gotbomb, tennis the next day with a real looker named Ladenia Blossom and depending on the weather, have a go at golf on Thursday with Phil Coffer who is the town mortician. Think he'll bury me?"

Patting his arm she said, "They're all good people. You'll enjoy them"

"Incidentally, I noticed that Ford and I would be playing bridge with the Gotbombs. Don't you like bridge?"

"Nah, I prefer Pinochle. Playing with the judge brings tears to my eyes."

"Oh no, don't tell me he's so good he takes all the fun out of it."

"Well, not exactly. It's just that------well, you'll see."

At that moment Ford appeared towing a lady by the hand. "Hey Horace, I want you to meet Henrietta Throckmorton, a very special friend of ours. She lives right at the entrance to the Upson Downes and no one, and I mean no one who doesn't belong here, gets by her and her mastiff, Buttons."

Horace was startled by anyone having a mastiff named Buttons and also felt the lady's description was hardly flattering, but she threw her head back in laughter. With that she tucked her arm through Horace's as she led him away. Obviously not having heard his name properly she said, "Bink Bottom, that's so formal. In order for me to remember names anymore, I have to keep them on a short tether. Would you mind if I call you Binky?"

Horace was surprised she missed his visible wince at the prospect of being called Binky, and in the many introductions she led him through, he did try to interject his proper name, but to no avail. He had to admit that being squired about the room by Throcky, as she asked him to call her, was an adventure. With a Mae West figure, extraordinary green eyes, peaches and cream complexion, frizzy silver hair and an almost non-existent chin, she was a sketch.

When it was time to leave, she said, "Why don't you come by my house in the morning and meet Buttons? I'll brew up the coffee and whip up a batch of sticky buns,"

"Invitation accepted," he said.

Chapter 4

ASIDE FROM THE FACT THAT sticky buns were a favorite of his, Horace was dying to meet a mastiff named Buttons. His ring of Throcky's doorbell the next morning triggered a frenzy of hysterical barking which immediately erased *mastiff* and substituted *rodent* for what he was about to encounter.

When she opened the door the smaller of the two occupants squirted out to sample his ankles. He wouldn't have classified himself as an unkind person, but being used to hunting dogs he found he would have no qualms about relegating this hysterical cucaracha to the end of a hor-d'oeuvre skewer.

Picking up the frothy saucer-eyed organism she scolded, "No no, you naughty thing. Be nice to this man."

From the snippy growls that continued in his direction as they went down the hall, he was sure the phrase, *nice man*, was mere fodder to this creature.

To him, the room they entered fit Throcky to a tee. Scattered with pieces of comfortable overstuffed furniture in orange and yellow floral patterns, the sense of hominess was immediate. Randomly placed throw rugs were scattered around a highly polished oak floor and a trio of tasteful Parisian prints above a large stone fireplace framed on either side by shelves stuffed with books completed the picture. On one side of the room a graceful arched window offered a view of the cove at the end of a sloping grassy area surrounded by a variety of birch and aspen trees.

Throcky was easy to talk to and in the course of their conversation that covered everything from politics to the outrageous price of gasoline, he also learned that before retiring she had held the position of high school principal in a small Missouri town and during that time had played first base for a woman's softball team. He asked, "Did you ever play professionally?"

"But of course. I always played professionally. We had a wonderful team and the gal who started the league had at one time been a stripper. At her suggestion we called ourselves *The Bosom Butties*."

"Are you serious?" asked Horace who had almost dropped his coffee cup on that one.

"Yes, but it's amazing how many people have no sense of humor. In fact some were quite offended so we changed the name to the *Wind Bags.*"

"And that was better?

"Apparently, because we blew everybody away," she said with a raucous laugh.

Aware that Buttons had been monitoring his every move he felt he should bestow some recognition on this minute quadruped and asked how long she'd had him.

She picked up and nuzzled the fur ball. "I've had him a couple of years. My sister gave him to me. "We flew home on a big plane didn't we Buttons? He traveled in a very special place."

"How in the world did you get him past all that patting down and groping they do?"

She reddened slightly as she said, "He wasn't on me. My sister had this small Cloisonne box with tiny holes in it, so we had him lightly sedated, put him in the box and I took it as carry-on luggage."

'He still had to go through the scanner didn't he?"

"Well yes, and that caused a problem. The girl watching the scanner let out a whoop and people came running from everywhere One security guard said the picture looked like a couple of fried eggs on a bed of rat skeleton. Imagine saying such a thing about my precious Buttons."

Almost falling off his chair in anticipation Horace asked, "So what happened next?"

"They gave me a very stern lecture, then, since Buttons was still so sedated, they charged me a fee and let me keep the box with him in it."

Noting that a couple of hours had quickly passed, he thanked Throcky for her wonderful stories, good coffee and sticky buns superior to any he'd ever eaten. Aware that Buttons was watching him with all the ennui of a crocodile at feeding time, he carefully sidled his way to the door. On an impulse he said, "Hey, I'm in the mood for a barbecue. How about next Tuesday evening? I'll call the Pickups and we'll make it a celebration."

Her face lit up. "I just knew you were my kind of guy but what are we celebrating?"

"Who needs a reason?

Chapter 5

HOME FROM THROCKY'S, HORACE CALLED the Pickups. "How about coming to a barbecue Tuesday night? Throcky's already a taker and we'd love to have you two join us."

"Sounds great, what can we bring?" Dotson asked.

"Just you're lovely company. Throcky's going to make a little something or other to nibble on."

"Well, that tall drink of water I'm married to likes a special beer so I'll have him bring his own. Sounds fun. We'll be there"

Horace was looking forward to finally entertaining for fun. The evenings were still too cool to be on the deck and when he heard Ford would be late because of school crossing duty he suggested the girls come early and spend some quality time in the hot tub.

When Ford did arrive, he frowned, gave a look around and said, "Where are the girls? I don't hear a sound."

Horace gestured toward the hot tub. "They've been quiet as mice."

"My gawd, if that contraption can keep things this silent, I'm getting one tomorrow. We've plenty of room in the garage," Ford said.

"The sales lady told me some people actually turn their tubs into fish ponds."

"If you're talking about Amanda Reversnuck, I could fish all day if she was the catch," Ford said with a laugh. "Say Horace, there's a gal for you. Sweet as all get out, smart as a whip and pretty as a picture."

"I've already checked and she's taken."

"Well in the words of my grandson, DUH, she's not married yet," Ford countered.

"True"

Horace was grateful that Ford in his quiet way sensed it was a subject Horace didn't wish to pursue. Instead, he got busy opening his beer and stretching out on a chaise when he said, "Ya know what? I bet if you did make that tub into a pond the fish would drink less wine and eat fewer Hors d' ouvres than those two gals."

"As far as the Hors d' ouvres are concerned, Throcky brought a bunch and they are delicious," said Horace.

Settling across from each other Horace brought up a subject he'd been curious about. "Tell me Ford, I've been trying to picture Dotson behind the wheel of one of those eighteen wheelers you told me that the two of you drove around the country. She's small enough to get lost in a lint trap. How in the world did she drive one of those?"

Leaning over, Ford whispered, "She didn't have the steering wheel in her hands, but she did the driving."

Rocking back in laughter Horace said, "Oops sounds like my mother."

"It sure was a great way to see the country and we met some wonderful people All was well until those cozy nights in the sleeper cab produced an Edsel. I'm still havin' trouble with that kid. When our girl came along we knew it was time to put down some roots. When I told my employers I was leavin' they offered me a job in the office. Two years later I bought the darn company, but by then I was thinkin' about retiring. We were in the southern part of the state and just for somethin' to do, we opened up a used car lot. Called it the Lemon Grove."

With a hoot, Horace said, "What a name for a car lot."

"Yeah, we had a money back guarantee that had a time limit of course, but if the car didn't work to their satisfaction, they could return it, no questions asked. I was head mechanic and every car left our lot in tip top shape. Never had to put my money where my mouth was."

"Ford, you're the only guy I know who could get away with something like that."

Rising to check the ribs, Horace said, "Hey, if you'll round up that pod of whales over in the pond these ribs will be served the minute the gals are dressed."

Licking a finger as she was finishing dinner, Throcky said, "Best ribs I've ever eaten. You ought to bottle the sauce."

"Can't, it's an old and secret family recipe," Horace said.

"No kidding, these are fabulous. Say, I'm head of the barbecue at the club the end of this month. How about earning your angel wings and doing ribs like this for us?" Ford said.

"Wait a minute, an expert I'm not", stated Horace.

"I beg to differ with you. Last year some yokel from town did it and not only were the ribs so tough they were inedible, whatever he slathered on them must of come off the bottom of a----

"Ford, mind your mouth," scolded Dotson.

"Well," Horace said, "I'll try, but since I'm the new kid on the block I'd feel better if you'd help me in the kitchen, or at least advise me where to buy the meat."

With a holler Dotson said, "That would be a mighty big mistake. He doesn't buy meat unless it's still wiggling, slithering or barking back."

After coffee in the den Horace started to pour another cup for Throcky who declined, saying, "I'd better get home to Buttons. I didn't give him much supper and I hate to think what he might be trying to devour in retaliation."

The Pickups left too and Horace had just settled down with a cup of coffee and some soft music to savor the evening when the phone rang. He saw it was a call from his mother and because it was so late, he was slightly alarmed. "Mother, are you alright?

In an excited voice she said, "Horace I've decided to take you up on your offer and bring my bridge group over."

"Now? It is after midnight Mother."

"I didn't mean tonight silly, but I wanted to let you know as soon as possible. Several of the ladies have expressed an interest in not only seeing your home but taking a dip in your hot tub. Why they have any interest in that I haven't the foggiest. Frankly, it's mind boggling to imagine any of them out of full dress."

Horace couldn't help but laugh. That's fine Mother. How about next Monday? I'll provide the refreshments and you bring the entertainment."

Chapter 6

HORACE SAID TO THE BUTCHER, "Sir, you sure know how to select meat. I'm very pleased with my order of ribs."

"Thank you. I actually learned meat selection from my dad."

"You're kidding. So did I. When I think about all the things I learned from my Dad I must say he left me an incredible legacy."

Handing Horace his packages of meat the butcher giving a thumbs up said, "Couldn't have said it better myself. Enjoy."

Elated, Horace was thoroughly enjoying the ride home. The top on his Miata was down and he was soaking up one of those beginning of spring days when the sight of trees and bushes alive with new foliage, indicated the eviction notice had been served on the last traces of winter's now dull blanket.

As he rounded the sun-laced curve that began the ascent to his place he nearly skidded to a halt. There was a creature of odd extraction rooting about in Throcky's garden. As he inched forward the creature rose on its haunches and he saw it was the old girl herself. Out of relief he gave a toot on his air horn that catapulted the lady into her freshly planted delphiniums. "Hi Throcky, see you tonight," he hollered.

Once his packages were unloaded, he started puttering around the kitchen putting his recipe together. Lamenting to himself that he should write the ingredients down so he'd at least have a clue what he'd done before he finally got the marinade to finger lickin' good. Once done, he did chill his decanter of Martinis to take with him. He rued that the presence of such a delicate delight had to be hidden in a decanter in order to assuage the sensitivities and narrow perception of some of the ladies who felt that the appearance of bottles on the tables led to overindulgence. Once done with his chores he went off to play tennis.

That evening, the crowd arriving at the club house seemed to have been infused with the hint of spring in the air and everyone was in a festive mood. Turning at a tap on his shoulder he encountered Teenut Boltrite whom he'd just finished playing tennis with. "My, my, don't we look spiffy and color coordinated to boot. Blues and grays and saddle shoes too. Are those back in style or am I lookin' at leftovers?

"A little bit of both," Horace assured him.

Teenut was a nickname he'd made up from his first and middle names of Tyree Nutting Boltrite and to Horace, the name Teenut Boltrite, was about as musical sounding as Horace Binkbottom.

Teenut, was a shy and quiet man with a magnificent head of bright red hair atop his tall and lean figure. His manner belied his tenacity on the tennis court, a game he'd taken up after retirement to, as he put it, "Avoid being run over in the house by the little woman." His wife had died five years ago. He'd spent most of his life working with construction companies, "But" he always emphasized, "I was an estimator. The only thing I ever constructed was a barn out of an erector set I got for Christmas when I was a kid."

With a jolt as he turned to leave Teenut, Horace bumped into Throcky.

"Binky, she exclaimed as she gave him an enthusiastic hug. "You and that abominable air horn. I have an ultimatum for you. Don't be surprised if someday you find that thing stuffed where it will make the most music."

With a sweeping bow Horace said, "Madam, I meant no offense, but tell me, what is that stunning gown you are wearing. I can never remember what they're called. Did you make it yourself?"

"It's a Caftan, and surely sir you jest when you ask if I made it. I can't find a needle much less the hole to put the thread in. If it weren't for the abundance of second time around shops in this neck of the woods, I'd be clad only in my glasses and don't see to well out of those. I do resemble a rainbow in search of a pot, but it does hide the peaks and valleys."

Turning away with a laugh Horace's drink did get sloshed when he backed into a total stranger. "I'm so sorry. Hope I didn't get you wet. Horace Binkbottom's the name, and to whom am I speaking?"

"Zack Finney here, retired Captain U.S. Navy Submarine Service," he rumbled.

Recoiling from the rumble, as much as from the vise like hand shake, Horace asked, "Are you new here? I don't believe I've seen you around."

"I dropped anchor a week ago. Call this lovely place home-port now."

Attempting to avoid any entanglement in the lanyards of navy lingo, and with an eye to a future game partner he asked, "Do you by any chance play golf?"

Lowering his voice almost to a whisper Zack said, "Always wanted to, but my wife bless her, whichever part of heaven she might be flapping around in, thought anyone who chased an insignificant white ball around six acres of grass looking for a hole to knock it into had to be a pea brain."

Horace felt he was in the sights of a just launched torpedo dead on target when the Captain added, "Bet you play."

"Oh, I just play for fun and exercise."

"Good chap. I like that approach. How'd you like to teach me? Looking at his watch he proclaimed, "It's seventeen-thirty-hours now. We'll rendezvous at the clubhouse at o-eight hundred tomorrow morning."

Beginning to feel like a leaky row boat in the path of a hurricane, Horace was startled by the jarring clap on his shoulder by Zack, who'd finished this proclamation and was saying conspiratorially, "Now Binkbottom, let's get down to serious business. Why don't you introduce me to some of these lovely females."

Horace figured that Throcky was the only person he knew who could take the wind out of the captain's sails and make him like it.

"Follow me," he said to the captain when he'd spied Throcky across the room. After introducing Zack he said, "Captain, I'm sorry but I have the duty tonight, however this lovely lady will take good care of you and I'll see you on the golf course at o-eight-hundred tomorrow morning.

As he walked away he heard Throcky saying, "So, you're a Captain. Well, not to worry. We all make mistakes."

Ford as promised was already out by the grill to help Horace with his duties. They got the fire going, spread the ribs over the coals and settled back to wait. Ford, opening a can of his favorite libation asked, "Getcha a whistle wetter?"

"No thanks, I'm all set."

"Hey, that's a slick way to carry your goodies around. I could pack myself a good wallop in one of those and the little woman would never know. She'd think I was drinkin' coffee."

"Ford, I didn't know you'd never seen my decanter before, but don't think you could ever fool Dotson with something like this. That's one smart lady you have. Incidentally, I didn't see her out front. Is she okay?"

"Oh yeah. When I left home she was still all a-twitter over one of those moldy salads she likes to make."

With a laugh Horace said, "I think the term is molded salad."

"Moldy, molded, they all look alike to me. Say, did your mother's bridge group ever come up to your place?'

"Oh my God yes. It was awesome. This troupe of little old ladies came traipsing up to my front door with arms at half mast like a platoon of doctors going into surgery. That sterile atmosphere survived the first glass of sherry and then all kinds of interesting things began to happen. Two of them had already donned bathing suits and tip-toed into the pool. Trouble was, one of them was flitting about in water wings and the other one was wearing an inner-tube. Needless to say, they took up most of the space but some of the others slid in too so they were really packed in there. My mother was right when she said that imagining any of them out of full dress was mind-boggling."

Ford said, "I sure wish I'd been there and had a camera."

"Oh, that wasn't the best part," Horace said. "My mother had also asked me to remove my bronze alligator from the front walk as she felt that would be a turnoff for some of the ladies, so what I did was park it in the bushes by the hot tub, and I wired a couple of red lights where its eyes were and once the tub was full I dimmed the room light and lit up the crocodile. Man, what a shrieking exit. Needless to say I gave the hot tub a good scrubbing after that."

At that moment Dotson, clad in a coral colored sheath with stunning floral designs in pinks, whites and tans, swung through the door under full steam. "I might have known I'd catch you two reprobated loafin' away back here. Anytime I don't see that husband of mine around all I have to do is look where the food is cookin'. Don't burn those ribs Ford. They smell heavenly, but hurry up. Everyone's gettin' antsy."

"Dotson" said Horace, "You look like a fresh picked bouquet of flowers,"

"Don't sweet talk me good lookin'. Flowers die if they're not fed properly, so tell me, will this masterpiece be done in our lifetime or should I get on the horn and order pizza?"

"Okay, pretty lady. Just put those platters over here because we're ready to roll."

To Horace's relief, the ribs were a huge success and he was asked many times for the recipe. This request was politely declined under his often repeated excuse of "To tell you the truth, I honestly don't remember". By now he'd come to think of this recipe as his ace in the hole. Where his marinade went, he went.

Teenut congratulated him on his grocery selection then said, "Say, I heard through the grapevine that you've offered to teach that new guy Zack somethin' or other how to play golf. That's a pretty tall order."

"Is your appraisal in reference to his size physically and vocally, or to my lack of expertise on the golf course?"

"Neither of the above, but I hear he's a national hero of sorts as well as a Captain. Sure hope your golf's better than your tennis." At the crestfallen look on Horace's face he said, "Hey, I'm sure he won't be a problem for you."

Horace said, "Well by tomorrow night I'll know just how good or bad it went. When it's all over I'll call you with a blow-by-blow description. By then I'll need someone to talk to."

Chapter 7

THE NEXT MORNING HORACE'S HEART sank when he saw a rather odd blotch of jarring color coming up the path to the Pro-shop. He really couldn't make out what, or who it was, until he was assailed by the familiar greeting "Ho Binkbottom, here I am ready to go, cleats and all."

All of a sudden, the ruddy face above floral patterned shirt and shorts which hung like limp drapery around white spindly moose like legs did a lot to burst Horace's bubble of anxiety. Further diminishing this bubble was the sight of his flat bottom and slim hips. He marveled that the lower portion of the man was able to support the muscular top half, with its barrel chest and broad shoulders. "By George, anyone who has guts enough to dress like that can't be too stuffy," he told himself.

Pointing to a pair of vintage football shoes draped around his neck Zack said, "I wasn't sure if my old size elevens would suffice, but the Yo-Yo in the pro shop set me on course and sold me these beauties" he said, holding out a foot.

Though he'd felt obliged to compliment Zack on his attire, he couldn't quite block out the startled stares of passer-bys. Horace preferred to walk the course, but for this occasion he had rented a cart in case it should become necessary to rapidly vacate wherever they might be.

Once underway, he decided to stop by the driving range and putting green first, in order to acquaint Zack with the bag of hardware he was toting around. After going over some of the rudiments like grip, stance, swing, different clubs and their uses he suggested that Zack take a few practice swings.

The big fellow hesitated, then sorted out a club, rearranged himself over an imaginary ball, and came through with a mighty slice, the sound of which was not unlike that of a jet plane going by at low altitude.

"Good, good. Let's get right over to the course". When they arrived he said, "Count down's over captain, fire when ready."

"Oh no. Not me. You go first and I'll pick up some pointers."

"Well, okay. Just remember to always check your grip and body position, keep that left arm rigid, head down and club face to the ball."

The shot that Horace came through with startled him to the core. He said with wonder as he shaded his eyes to track his shot, "Wow, I didn't even hear the ball leave the tee."

One moose-like knee across the other as he leaned on his club Zack said stonily, "It didn't."

Reddening Horace mumbled, "Oh, wow. It sure can't make any sound if you don't connect with it" he said, and came through with a second shot straight down the fairway. "Okay, your turn."

After the fifth hole, Horace had to admit the Captain had a very unique swing. What usually started out like a weed eater, almost always turned into a bulldozer effect as he always managed to dislodge a large chunk of turf to which his ball and tee were still attached.

Horace replaced the turf as best he could then suggested that, since this hole wasn't much of a challenge, they might as well mosey along to the next one. The captain's stance on this one was, to Horace, not unlike that of a Samurai warrior about to behead an opponent. He closed his eyes, said a silent prayer and heard the unmistakable crack of the club hitting the ball and a bellow of, "Thar she blows!" from Zack.

Noting that the ball, tee and chunk of the grass had left the premises he asked in pleased wonderment, "Where".

"Ah no," came Zack's disappointed answer "It's in that foxhole over there."

"That's called a bunker, and not to worry, it happens to best of us."

After several minutes of Zack reducing the bunker to a well bombed beachhead, and Horace tallying up the cost of bringing in a skip-load of sand, suggested they cheat a little and put Zack's ball up on the fairway. As they stood aside for the umpteenth group to play through, 'Zack, looking at his watch said, "Seems to me we've been gone long enough to warrant the arrival of the Saint Bernards. I sure could use a generous portion of first aid and something to ease my blisters."

"Hang in there Zack, we've only got two more holes to go."

Sitting down on the edge of the bunker Zack said, "Aw, forget it. I think my wife was right when she said only pea brains chase these crazy little balls around. Anyway, if I'd known I'd be spending so much time playing in the sand I would have brought a bucket and spade."

Somehow this small boy bit of exasperation exposed a soft spot in this blustery sea captain that melted some of Horace's own futility. At that moment his ball came flying out of a hole in the sand followed by a furry, bright eyed and very irate gopher. It eyed the two men in disgust, retreated into its hole and threw out three more balls.

This brought a tension breaking loud laugh from both of them, and did wonders for Zack's next shot that went straight down the fairway toward the ninth green. Now, with his face aglow beneath his swatch of white hair and his posture once again that of a man in charge, he took aim and swung.. From the crack of club against ball Horace knew this was far and away the Captains best shot of the day.

However, his excitement waned when the ball instead of stopping on the green, continued its flight with a graceful arch above the low trees along the railing of the clubhouse outside dining porch, bounced once and dropped neat as a pin into a drink Ladenia Blossom was raising to her lips.

Horace felt a strong urge to take up life behind the nearest tree and was utterly dumbfounded when he saw Zack sputter his way to the porch and make his self known as the perpetrator of this mishap.

Ladenia was a lady Horace had met at his first home owners meeting and played tennis with the next day. Since then he had spent many a Friday evening as her bridge partner and enjoyed her immensely. She was petite, vivacious, and yet unpretentious considering the comfort zone she coasted in from the sale of her late husband's plumbing conglomerate. Her large brown eyes, always sparkling with mischief, were framed by silvery short hair brushed like a halo around her face. She was one of those people who could look stunning wearing a gunnysack. Obviously having just come from the tennis courts, her tanned figure, clad in smart white shorts and tank top was unnervingly attractive.

In one of our Friday night chats she had revealed to Horace how she chose her husband to be. "I was an elevator operator. That was when one sat in the corner to run the thing. It was right across from the men's room and he was the only man who came out of there who didn't need tidying up."

It crossed Horace's mind that if anyone had to be the *victim* in this present situation, Ladenia was probably the one who could take it in stride.

He could hear Zack saying, "My dear lady, I'm terribly sorry. Here, here, let me help." He unfurled from the back pocket of his shorts a handkerchief the size of a dishtowel. With this he proceeded to mop up the table.

Just as Horace arrived, Ladenia was plucking from her cleavage, a piece of pineapple that had sailed there from her Mai Tai, when it was replaced by Zack's golf ball.

On spotting Horace she exclaimed with relief, "Binky, what are you doing here? Did you see what just happened?"

"I did and I must say it was the Captain's best shot of the day because he got to meet you."

This explanation had the effect of the world grinding to a halt, and looking at Zack she cooed, "Ooooooh, a Captain. Didn't I see you at the barbecue last night?" "In person," Zack breathed in a whisper.

Horace reluctantly interrupted their foggy interlude and asked, "Ladenia, may I get you another drink?"

His question had the same effect on Zack as if he'd been shot out of a cannon. Jumping up he bellowed to the nervous waiter, "Bring three more of the same here, and while you're at it bring a round for everyone on the porch."

With a magnanimous bow he said to the everyone on the porch who were staring at this scene with mouths agape like a school of carp at feeding time, "Sorry for the interruption folks." With that he sat down again and returned his full attention to Ladenia's warm gaze.

After trying to get in a word here and there, Horace finally gave up and rose to leave. No one heard his excuses and when he looked back Zack was going full tilt on his submarine adventures while a somewhat cross-eyed Ladenia, a small parasol from her drink tucked behind one ear was cooing, "Really? How brave you were."

Once he reached home and folded his sun baked and weary frame into the comfortable padding of a lounge chair on his deck, Horace gratefully took a sip if his cold drink. This along with the strains of one of the Manheim Steamroller's romantic recordings was going a long way toward easing his pain.

As he watched the gold disc of sun sink behind the purple haze of distant mountains, the tranquility of the moment brought Amanda to mind. When she wasn't too busy he would stop and chat with her, but now that winter was over and sales were picking up, those moments were rare. He'd heard that a group of ladies in the community were planning a bridal shower for her.

He finally made his promised call to Teenut with an update on the golf game with Zack. After listening s few moments to some of the things that had happened, Teenut said, "Wow, sounds like he let go with a few torpedoes."

"It was more like an excavation." Horace said. "I'm, not sure what to do. It is my responsibility. My biggest worry is all the lost divots. The course looks like it had been bombed."

In his usual calm manner his friend said, "Horace, no point in worryin' about it. Grass is like hair. It grows back."

Chapter 8

THE RINGING OF THE TELEPHONE one morning jarred Horace into an annoyed and sleep filled "Hullo." From the sound of his voice he knew that recovery from the previous night's foray into Zack's version of a military punch would be hard to overcome. Their friendship had flourished with subsequent golf games, plus the discovery that what he had mistaken as pomposity and brashness in the man masked a loneliness he'd battled since the loss of his wife.

"Mr. Binkbottom? Cookie Nowall here. I hope it's not too early for a call, but I'm on the committee in charge of the CPR course that's going to be given at the clubhouse and we need some volunteers," trilled an unfamiliar voice.

Horace came close to a shout when he asked, "Volunteers for what? I'm not the least bit interested in being the sacrificial lamb on a demonstration table."

With a giggle Cookie Nowall said, "No, no, that's not what we need. We want a few people to help recruit the audience. You know, talk up the program so we have a good turnout."

In a cloud of gloom Horace said, "Well, can you tell me a little more about the subject matter and how it is going to be presented?"

As it turned out Cookie could tell him less than he already knew, but did manage to gush through the phone that "Mrs. Forecliff, who is considered to be one of the best in the CPR business, is going to be our demonstrator."

It was with reluctance that Horace finally agreed to spread the gospel according to Cookie Nowall. Since door to door confrontation was not one of his strong suits, the first occasion he had to launch his lofty missionary goal came as he and Ford Pickup were having a committee meeting of sorts, on the most economical way to resurface and repaint the tennis courts.

"After all Ford, I'm sure we'd both hope that if we ever needed these life saving procedures, we'd be able to count on the givee with a heavy thumb on our life's balancing scale, to have some clue as to what the heck they were supposed to be doing."

"It's not that I'm against it, I'm just uncomfortable with what is required to learn it. Besides, I don't think I could ever breathe down a perfect stranger's mouth. It doesn't seem sanitary to me."

"Ho, ho, I got you there, buddy. They no longer do that. The new procedure is using chest compressions. It's a big step forward. Anyway, you've talked about how worried you get that something might happen to your grand-kids when they come to visit in the summer. Knowing some of these procedures might ease your mind."

"I've got that one already figured out. When they come I'm going to tether them to some Helium balloons, and lower em' down only at feeding time."

"Over my dead body, you old reprobate. I'm signing up right now," said Dotson as she joined them.

"I might have known I'd get caught. Guess I'd better sign up too, if only in self defense," said Ford.

After the Pickups had agreed to attend he found it easier to line up other recruits. His chance to nail Throcky, came a couple of days later when he and Zack overtook her on the golf course. She was floundering through a round with her niece and said, "Glad you came along. I need a breather. My personal definition is that this game is strictly push and shove. She pushes her bag around with three clubs in it, and I shove mine about with enough stuff to open a pro-shop. Want to buy a club or two?"

"No thanks, but I would like your cooperation."

After explaining his mission Throcky said, "Count me in. Any chance I might get to practice on you Binky? Might be I could give you a second start. I mean, at your age you must surely have hidden talents other than playing the air horn on that kiddie car Miata you call an automobile."

"What a terrible way to speak of the woman I love," he replied with a laugh.

"Well, you ought to find a sleeker model, for instance, take my niece, she's----"

"I'd love to," Horace said, smiling over at the tall willowy blond girl.

"Enough" scolded Throcky. "You've made your point. Now scoot on through so I'm not embarrassed when I sail my ball into yon pond."

The only person on his list who he hadn't caught up with was Ladenia Blossom. He met up with her as she came out of the clubhouse. She had just left the aerobics class and as always looked striking in a white trimmed turquoise sweat suit.

With an amused expression she said, "Dr. Livingston I presume. I've heard about your mission and yes, I intend to be there. I've always felt one can't learn too much about emergency procedures. Wish I could apply it to myself though. Some mornings I need a blast just to get out of bed."

Horace was pleased at the large turnout for the class. As usual, among the uninformed, a few words will often make their way to the fore and cause distress for some. In this case the words being bandied about were *practice on each other.*

Zack's arrival turned out to be the lantern in the dark, so to speak. He sloughed the problem aside and shifted everyone's concerns into neutral, when he told them, "You will not be called upon to participate in any public demonstration if you don't wish to. In most cases they use dummies."

"You didn't tell me you'd volunteered," quipped Ladenia. This brought a loud guffaw from Zack and the audience. Though their relationship still had trial balloon stamped on it, they had become a tentative twosome since the golf ball in the Mai Tai incident.

Horace had bitten into an almond tidbit from the cookie tray and had exhaled in laughter at her remark. He inhaled again at the sight of an absolutely Amazonian sized lady who had barged through the door. He assumed this must be Mrs. Forecliff, the instructor. She had tightly curled mousy brown hair, bright rosy cheeks and intense black eyes. Over her arm was draped a limp and dangly half of another lady, obviously the victim. This poor creature she flung on the table like a slab of meat. The whole interaction caused Horace to inhale and choke on a nut from a cookie he'd just bitten into. This caused Mrs. Forecliff to zero in on his strangled sounds.

At that moment Teenut, who was in the chair next to Horace let go with a hefty thwack to his back. This dislodged the nut which propelled forward and found refuge in the lace collar of Mrs. Snowberry's dress.

Horace had heard about Mrs. Snowberry but had never met her formally. He understood that her dead husband had left her a fortune to wallow around in that purportedly matched her size; considerable on both counts. He had also been told that she was a dominant force in community activities and the sort one doesn't mess about with. For those reasons Horace didn't feel the circumstances warranted an introduction on his behalf. To tap a perfect stranger on the shoulder and say, "Pardon me but my nut is entangled in you collar." Where does one go from there? Besides he was too busy trying to become invisible to the behemoth headed in his direction.

"No! No! No," she bellowed.

With a hooked finger that could have landed a marlin Mrs. Forecliff beckoned to Teenut, not Horace, and said, "Come up front with me young man. Don't ever do to anyone else, what you just did to that gentleman."

Relief spread over Horace like a down comforter as he watched unlucky Teenut rise slowly and bob behind the lady.

He ran into her when she stopped suddenly and in his shy manner explained, "It seemed the quickest thing to do. He was making an awful racket."

Eyeing him like he was a piece of bait she said, "No matter. You can do more harm than good, if you pound someone on their back. It could force whatever the object is, farther down their throat."

With that she spun him around and encased him in her huge arms. Placing a fist the size of a boxing glove between his navel and rib cage, she grabbed that fist with another of equal size and said, "This is how you properly clear a windpipe." That said, she gave a mighty upward thrust. What she dislodged, was a mammoth belch from the bug eyed Teenut. Dusting off her hands, she said, "It's good for that too." Un-spinning the hapless fellow she discarded him as though he was a newspaper headed for the recycle bin.

This unique lady then launched into what had to be her favorite subject. Her explanation of the short time lapse in which brain damage can occur caused several sharp intakes of breath. Droning on she said, "You will see just how useful this technique can be in a life-threatening situation. However, it also has a down side. If improperly used, damage could occur."

That statement had just enough impact to shift the game to a different ballpark as several people, Horace included, ogled each other in an attempt to assess whether anyone they knew would be worth the stress that would occur if it turned out that someone else's demise was at their hands.

Suddenly aware of the noxious weed she had inadvertently planted with that warning, Mrs. Forecliff invited the audience up to the table to watch the demonstration."First off, you should quickly assess whether your victim is still breathing. The chest should be rising one and one-half to two-seconds per breath."

Moving right along she continued, "For nearly 40 years, CPR guidelines have trained people to tilt the victim's head back to open the airway, pinch their nose and deliver several breaths into their mouth. They have found however, that instead of that, it is far better to do a series of chest compressions. The only mistake anyone can make is to not respond immediately to the situation. Compressions pump blood to the victim's brain and heart while delivering needed oxygen. They should be delivered at approximately100 per minute until help arrives."

After a hearty round of applause Mrs. Forecliff called out, "C'mon now, don't be bashful. You're all welcome to try out on my model here."

She might as well have been speaking to a morgue full of cadavers. No one moved. Quickly scanning the room her memory laser honed in on Horace and Teenut. Almost on their knees, they hurriedly scooted out the door. "Wow, what a technique," Horace said.

"Yeah, but I hate to think what would have come out if she'd used her technique on me one more time."

"Hey teenut, I think you made a highly definitive statement, but I'll say one thing. If I ever need CPR I hope Mrs. Forecliff or someone like her is available to help me."

Chapter 9

HORACE HAD JUST FINISHED DRESSING for the spring dance at the clubhouse that night when the phone rang. It was his mother. Their conversations had grown in length and proportion to their developing relationship and there was no mistaking the excitement in her voice. "Horace, I'm going on a world cruise."

"That's wonderful mother. Are you going alone or is this one of those madcap things you and your bridge cronies do?"

"No, I'm going alone. I feel like getting away from it all, at least for awhile.'

"Let's have dinner before you go and you can tell me all about it."

After his mother had hung up he donned his tuxedo jacket and headed for the clubhouse. Pulling into one of the few parking spaces left, as he went to open *his* door, the car door of the auto parked next to him also opened and a ponderous lady struggled to get out. He hopped out and went around to help her. It was Mrs. Snowberry, the lady whose lace collar had given shelter to his nut when he discharged it at the CPR demonstration.

"Thank you, young man. They make cars so low these days one needs a crane to get in or out." Peering more closely at Horace she said, "I don't believe we've met."

My name is Horace Binkbottom, and you are Mrs. Snowberry. I've heard so much about you and your work here in the community."

"It's not much, but it does keep me out of mischief," she said with a giggle. Still looking puzzled she said, "I don't think I've seen you at any of our functions have I?"

"As a matter of fact I attended the CPR class this morning."

"That was marvelous except for the distraction of that poor creature behind me who had such a terrible choking spell. I thought for a moment we would have to have a live demonstration."

"Yes, yes, I agree. May I see you into the clubhouse?"

"No, I'm on KP duty. These days you can't trust people to do a simple job. I'm here to see that the caterers carry out their tasks properly."

Horace gave a small shudder on behalf of the caterers who were about to be tucked under Mrs. Snowberry's blanket of authority and headed into the clubhouse.

"There you are Mr. Binkbottom. It's so crowded we were wondering where we could put any more people. I believe you got the last seat in the house. Incidentally, I'm Cookie Nowall from the CPR committee. We did so appreciate your help."

Horace was stunned and had a hard time matching this attractive lady to the voice on the phone. She was cute as a button and reminded him of a pixie. She led him to a table occupied by Judge Gotbomb and his wife. This was the couple Ford and he had played bridge with one evening soon after Horace's arrival at Upson Downse.

The judge was a short, paunchy, garrulous man whose unruly silver hair with its pronounced cowlick gave him the appearance of being in continual shock. Aside from his fame as a teller of tales drawn from his life on the bench, he was also an undisputed master at the card table. Bridge, as Ford and he had learned the night they played with the judge and his wife, was his forte. This ability was surpassed only by his flair for flatulence. During their first game, he recalled Dotson's words about how playing cards with the judge brought tears to her eyes.

On arriving at the dinner table set for three, he noticed it was in a discreet position beyond the potted palms, down-wind from the dance floor, and near an exit. On greeting them Horace remarked to Mrs. Gotbomb what a pleasure it was to see her again and she chirped back, "Please, call me Alvina. No need to be formal with us."

Horace remembered the admiration he'd felt for her as she remained steadfast by her husband's side while Ford and he excused themselves now and then for a breather. She provided a serene and dignified accessory to her husband's unique avocation.

A foot taller than the judge, she was as shapeless as he was paunchy. Plain features accented by high cheekbones, brown eyes and a narrow nose were framed by straight brown hair parted in the middle and drawn down each side of her face to a tight bun in the back.

They ordered drinks from a harried waitress who showed signs of having come under Mrs. Snowberry's direction and fell into a comfortable pattern of easy chit-chat. Since no intolerable emissions were escaping from the judge he began to feel that perhaps the night of the card game had been an off evening for him. As she had that night, Alvina acquiesced graciously to her husband's control of the conversation with silence and an expression of adoration.

Later, he couldn't recall what he'd said in reference to the judge's work but it created a terrible excitement in the man. This gave vent to an unmistakable odor. Taking Alvina by the hand he asked, "Care to dance?"

"Please," she gasped and they headed out the door to the porch and fresh air.

Horace had no wish to embarrass Alvina with any reference to what had just happened, but preferred instead to draw this shy creature out of her shell. It seemed to him that in just this short time her features had already taken on a luminescent quality that revealed a striking, warm and appealing woman behind her façade of plainness.

Sensitive to her timidity he thought it best not to burden the conversation with any heavy discussion such as the merits of the current best seller, or the delights of the Picasso print show at the local gallery, so in an attempt to keep things light he asked, "Did I understand you to say earlier that you and the judge came from the same town?"

"That's right," she chirped. "Our worlds were far apart though. I admired him from the start. I'd heard so much about him because he was famous in our town, but I didn't meet him until he gave a series of lectures on law at the university.

Surprised, Horace asked, "You were a law student?"

"Oh, no, I was a law professor."

With a gulp, Horace realized he was swimming in a deeper pool than he'd anticipated and it hadn't been his intention that this bud he'd chosen to nurture into a flower should become a full blown garden full of the judge's blossoms but, it was obvious that he dominated her greenhouse.

Before he could switch the conversation back on track she said with a breathless laugh, "He popped the question of marriage, right after we met, or, as he used to joke, he handed down his verdict. He came to dinner one night and over his stuffed cabbage he said, "Alvina, as you would say in Latin, we are a unique omnium gatherum, but our auras blend in perfect harmony. In my opinion our intent to spend the rest of our lives together would be accepted by any court in the world."

Horace, not being privy to lawyerese, wasn't quite sure what she'd said, but assumed it was all legal.

"But my curiosity is still piqued by you," he told her. "Becoming a teacher of law at a university must have taken years of schooling."

"I had majored in Latin and Greek philosophy and expected to teach those subjects, but out of the blue I got this crazy urge to study law. Once into it, I found I didn't want to practice it, I wanted to teach it."

Horace, whirling her in a daring spin which she executed with flawless precision, bent his head as he said, "I beg your pardon, I didn't hear that last remark. I thought you made a comment."

It was then he became aware that they were in company with other than the sweet smell of night air and what he had heard, no matter how lady like had not been in Latin, Greek, or otherwise. He had to smile at the cohesive bond between these two people and his appraisal of the judge became quite conciliatory as he realized, his was not a solo act.

When the music came to a stop Horace said, "I have enjoyed our visit so very much, and I've been very selfish. I have a feeling I'd better get you back to your husband who must think I kidnapped you."

"In truth, I'd forgotten poor Jepson. By now he may have stewed away in his own juices and expired," she said.

Back at the table they found it empty. Looking around in concern Alvina said, "It's not like him to just up and disappear. I can't imagine where he could be."

"Perhaps he's on the dance floor," Horace ventured.

Their concerned glances turned to beguiled stares. The judge, wheezing loudly was pumping Throcky's hourglass shape through the gyrations of a Latin dance.

"I had no idea your husband was such an accomplished dancer".

"He loves it. When we were first married we entered a jitterbug contest. Two of the contest judges fainted from excitement."

"I'm not surprised," said Horace.

"What is that?" Alvina almost shouted.

Horace, following her gaze saw that Throcky's enthusiastic flamenco like movements had revealed a dark, hairy object in the pit of her lily white arm.

"I know what it is," said Alvina, who had leaned out into the dance floor for a better look. "It's lint from her dress. It's warm in here and the perspiration has caused the lint to stick in her arm pit. It's becoming bigger. At this rate she's liable to end up with her whole dress under her arm."

It was apparent that Throcky, whose motions bordered on the flamboyant, was not aware of the birth of this evolution in her arm pit.

Thinking that further pursuance of this quaint event could only lead to terrible consequences, Horace stepped forward to intervene. It came as no surprise when his tap on the nearly apoplectic judge's shoulder startled him into a loud and redolent retort.

Throcky didn't miss a beat. "Oh, it's you Binky. Isn't this wonderful?" she said as he grabbed her on her next go-around and steered her toward the outside porch where he hoped the cool night air would encourage the thing to drop from under her arm. After a series of frenetic bobs and ducks, he was able to see that her pristine armpit was once more free of its untoward baggage.

As though an all clear call had been sounded, Horace and Throcky glided back on to the dance floor. A quick thinker had turned on the ceiling fans and the patrons had returned to that for which they had come----to dine and dance.

Turning at a tap on his shoulder he found Teenut in line to take over Throcky. Her only comment at the transfer was "What an odd smell."

Teenut stepped back with an injured look. "It wasn't me ma'am."

Horace felt he should at least say goodnight to the Gotbombs, his dinner companions. He found them preparing to leave. "Hey you two, you can't leave yet. The party has just begun".

"I am sorry. I did enjoy my time with you, but the judge says that this has been too much activity for him. He's plum run dry. I'd better get him home so he can recharge his batteries."

Bidding them goodnight at the door, Horace had to shake his head over this unique and lovable couple.

Chapter 10

BECAUSE NO ONE EVER KNEW what to expect at any of Ladenia Blossom's unique social rendezvous, Horace always accepted her invitations with delight and anticipation. This evening's soiree had been billed as a "Gregorian Chant" sing along. The invitation had specified BYOM. Bring your own monk.

Late to arrive because he'd seen his mother off on her around the world cruise, Horace wasn't too surprised to find everyone lolling around on large colorful cushions with their shoes off.

"Must I?" He asked, slipping out of his loafers.

"It's mandatory," Ladenia stated. "The only way you can feel the full power of the music is from the floor up, or so I've been told."

After what seemed like an eternity of listening to weird music with their eyes closed, Zack announced he was making a pilgrimage to the kitchen to bless a fresh round of drinks and say a few hail monk's over another platter of what he called "Those dinky little hors d'oeuvres that wouldn't even grow hair under the arms of a tadpole."

Ladenia waved him on and plunked down across from Horace. "Binky, when are you going to give up being a bachelor and settle down with a nice girl?"

"Oh please, you sound like my mother, besides I can't think of anyone off hand that I'm interested in."

"Well then, how come you spend so much time hanging around Amanda's office?"

"Do you have a spy network?"

"I have my resources, and another question. Why do you volunteer for so many things? If you'd learn to tether you philanthropic tendencies to allow more time for the good things in life, maybe you'd fall into some damsels trap."

"Actually I feel duty bound to nurture my philanthropic persuasions. The trick I've learned is to keep my ear tuned to the needs of our small colony and offer help before I get asked. My big hearted propensity is merely a ploy. Instead of being stuck on somebody's dull committee it allows me to handpick only the tasks I feel comfortable doing."

With a laugh she said, "You are a sly old fox."

The next morning, Horace's usually successful ploy at offering his services ahead of time, fell prey to unusual circumstances.

"Mr. Binkbottom?" purred Phil Coffer's sonorous voice over the phone. "Would you be in a position to help us out this morning? It won't take long."

"What's up?" he asked.

"As you know, I'm treasurer of the Home Owners Association and have to justify any expenditures. This includes approval from the residents for any projects we wish to allot funds for. The thing is, we've received three bids on enlargement of the pool room and the one we'd like to accept has a time limit and requires that letters of consent be delivered to, and signed by the residents, giving us authority to proceed. The thing is we need these letters signed as soon as possible."

Phil was a pleasant chap, married to Ladenia Blossom's sister, Delfinia. High rosy cheeks, baldhead and a benign countenance that contrasted sharply with his keen penetrating gaze, gave one the uneasy feeling that he'd been behind the door when humor was meted out. However, his looks fit his job. He was a local undertaker. One often told story was of the poor soul who'd tried to dip his oar in Phil's mirth pot. He'd come away the owner of two caskets and a large burial plot.

Almost as an after-thought Phil said, "You won't be alone. Ford Pickup and Teenut Boltrite are going to help out."

"That's a surprise. You couldn't have picked three people with more aversion to ringing doorbells, especially if it concerns any kind of a contentious issue," Horace added.

"I can assure you, as I did them, that the nature of this quest should not produce any major confrontations."

He'd been right, and the monthly newsletter announced a few weeks later that the requested use of funds for enlargement of the pool room had been approved by a large majority. To no one's surprise, some of the men displayed signs of serious bleeding at the time lapse involved before their pool room was ready again. However, within a few days they found a tourniquet to their wound had been applied under the auspices of Mrs. Snowberry and the women's bridge group who had agreed to '*share*' their space with the men.

The balloons of heartfelt joy at this generous bounty soon sprung leaks when it was learned the ladies offer came with the dreadful price tag. *No conversation* please.

This put a severe strain on the men since most of them couldn't lift an arm without an uncomplimentary remark or two. "It makes me feel like a little boy having to raise my hand for permission to go *toity*," snorted the always placid Teenut.

On the first evening of the '*trial run*' the men out of their own good will, had divested themselves of cigars, cigarettes, pipes and any drinks they had been nursing. This apparently paid off when much to their relief they were greeted warmly by the female share-givers. After a low-key interlude of civil pleasantries, the two diverse activities coasted off to a cautious start. To this day, Horace still didn't feel it was their fault that the 'silence' edict brought forth a bevy of strangled snorts reminiscent of a pigsty in rutting season.

This of course elicited from the women, raised eyebrows, scornful looks, wrinkled noses and loud sniffs that registered disapproval of the *alleged* scent of tobacco smoke that lingered on clothing. There was no doubt that these reactions were meant to remind the men in no uncertain terms that the favor of *sharing* they had tendered, was merely a seed that could be aborted at any time.

In a miscalculated move, Horace's cue stick swung in a wild arc away from the table and made connections with Mrs. Snowberry's beehive hairdo. The 'do' turned out to be a hairpiece and he watched in frozen fascination as it soared into the air and found a perch on the chandelier above the card table. This in turn created a paralyzing lull that descended on the room.

Horace had always taken great personal pride in his ability to deliver a meaningful and quick response to any given incident, so he reached up with his cue stick retrieved the hair piece and placed it back on Mrs. Snowberry's head. Patting it he said, "There you go baby."

In a silence akin to midnight in Death Valley and feeling his demise was imminent he sidled out the door as quickly as possible. There, he collided with a gaggle of men who had fled the premises in case any mayhem might occur, but still in viewing distance in case it did.

No one, Horace included, was surprised when the next day the men were informed that the offer to *share* their premises had been withdrawn by the women.

Chapter 11

HORACE FELT TERRIBLE, AND WAS consumed with guilt. Not only had he embarrassed Mrs. Snowberry beyond belief, he had annihilated the share program in its entirety. A few evenings later he was on the Pickup's deck staring at a skewer, laced with a piece of orange and a maraschino cherry in the tall cool something-or-other that Dotson had handed him, when Ford broke the silence. "You look lower than a flat tire. You still in a tizzy over that card room caper?"

"Yes, and I've got to make amends, but I just don't know what to do."

"Sometimes it's better to let things like that die a natural death, and I'll tell you something else. I don't think a simple apology would fly with that lady."

"Yeah," quipped Dotson. 'You have to be mighty careful what you say to that skittish bunch of females. But hey, why don't you invite the lady for a spin in that rubber ducky raft you bought", she suggested.

Leaping up he gave her a big hug. "You are my life saver. I could paddle her to that small island out in the bay for a fancy picnic, you know, chilled wine in crystal glasses, imported cheese, the whole nine yards."

"I was just kidding," said Dotson.

"My gawd man. Think about what you're saying. That would be like towing the Q-E2 with your raft," interjected Ford.

Horace became so enamored with this idea he went home, took careful measurements of his raft and determined it would indeed hold the bulk that was Mrs. Snowberry. Gaining access to the lady was another problem, however she reluctantly agreed to allow him a few minutes of her time at two that afternoon, and ended with, "And don't be late,"

Almost buried under a ton of roses, Horace rang her doorbell at precisely two-o-clock. It was answered immediately and as she filled the entire space with herself, he realized his negotiations would be conducted from where he stood.

"You know of course why I'm here," he mumbled, and when she offered no further help he stumbled on with his heartfelt expression of regret for the unfortunate and unintentional occurrence in the card room." This portion of his program was met with the alacrity of a spent rubber band, though she did take the flowers. His desperate swim against her tide of unforgiving attitude left little hope that his proposition would even be considered, but he went on to say, "I would be most pleased if by way of making up for this grievous incident, you would be my guest for a spin across the bay in my new raft."

To his surprise a faint glimmer of interest appeared in her frozen expanse and he hurried on to say, "With a picnic on that small island, provided by me, of course."

The change in her demeanor compelled him to step to the side as the melt down began, and he could scarcely believe his ears when she said, "I'd be delighted, but tell me, are rafts safe?"

"My dear lady, your safety and comfort would be first and foremost in my mind. Never would I propose such a venture if I felt there would be any personal danger to you. I can assure you beyond doubt, that a raft is one of the most invincible crafts made by man."

Those words put Horace in immediate danger of being overtaken by her ooze of clemency and he said in haste as he backed up, "If ten o'clock tomorrow morning fits into your schedule I'll see you then."

He raced home and called Ladenia with a frantic, "Help! I have to put together a fancy picnic lunch by ten tomorrow morning. What shall I serve?"

"Binky, you devil you. I already know about it. Come on over. I love helping people out of corners they've painted themselves into."

Horace was ticked that this bizarre episode in his life had hit the wireless so fast and he wondered how many other people were chortling about it. However his temper had cooled by the time he arrived at Ladenia's and found she'd already made out a menu designed to impress Mrs. Snowberry.

As they sat down she said, "In my opinion you need to provide a luncheon of understated elegance, with a sprinkle of small delightful surprises, but at the same time, bold enough to blow her knee highs off. For starters, how about dainty dishes of Liver Pate or Brie Cheese with slivered almond to spread on rice crackers. After that you whip out the main course. How does this sound? Pickled quail eggs stuffed with beluga caviar and a Belgian endive salad with, a very light vinegar and oil dressing. This of course would be served with a chilled Pouilly Fume wine."

"Ladenia you never cease to amaze me. You mean real quail eggs? I've never had one."

"I had no idea how un-enlightened you are. Come with me and I'll introduce you to a quail egg. That specialty market in town has them."

After they got in his car he leaned over and gave her a big hug. "Ladenia, you're a doll, but do you think this will be enough for a crowd as big as---I mean Mrs. Snowberry?"

"Trust me, she'll love it. If that's not enough she can always fix herself a peanut butter sandwich when she gets home."

The next morning, basking in a bubble of good will and confidence at his natty appearance in Levis, blue sneakers, blue blazer, just a hint of a red scarf at his neck and his yachtsman's cap at a rakish angle, he spun up to Mrs. Snowberry's house in his top down

Miata. She had opened her door in expectation of his *on time* arrival, and called out with a joyful shout, "Ten o-clock on the dot. Be right with you Captain." He was almost startled out of his sneakers at her persona packaged in a bright yellow sun-suit trimmed in elegant eyelet lace, the crowning glory of which was a floppy brimmed yellow bonnet in the shape of a witch's hat that caged her beehive hairdo. She reminded him of an Egyptian Pyramid.

For just one awful moment he realized he had measured the raft with care, but had failed to consider the logistical dilemma of introducing this large mass into his small car.

He hopped out, opened the door as wide as it would go and taking both her hands in his, as he looked her up and down said, with forced enthusiasm, "My my, Mrs. Snowberry, you are a veritable beam of sunshine."

She giggled with girlish pleasure as she worked her way back and forth like a corkscrew until with a loud *'there'*, she sank on to the seat. Horace winced with pain as his beloved car gave a loud groan and listed to one side like a wounded grebe. Somewhere in the midst of their light chatter as they limped along to the lake, the problem of how to extract her from his Miata crept into his mind with the force of a bulldozer running over an ant.

As they pulled to a stop it became apparent that a bee had not only hitched a ride, but was attempting to find a home in the leg ruffle of Mrs. Snowberry's sun-suit. Her frantic motions were accompanied by a loud shriek and she ascended into the air like a phoenix rising from the ashes. To his delight this activity occurred at the same time he opened the door for her, and out she sailed.

Noting she had dislodged the bee with her orbital ascent she now looked in perplexity around the dock. "Where's the raft?" she asked.

"Right down this way, my dear. Follow me."

"The two of us are going in that?" she asked in doubt and bewilderment.

"More than adequate," he assured her.

Taking her arm Horace said, "Once you're safe on that seat in the other end of the raft, I'll do the honors and we'll be off for a leisurely cruise and a scrumptious lunch."

Her confidence returned and she said, "Imagine, my first sail on the lake." Then with an upside down salute she snapped with vigor, "Ready when you are, Captain."

With Horace's assistance, Mrs. Snowberry stepped with boldness into the raft which immediately sank to a precarious level in the water. She then lurched to her designated post, turned and sat down on the inflated cushion.

Turning to climb in Horace found himself in a predicament he couldn't believe. His end of the raft was sticking up out of the water. After a few aborted attempts he managed to balance himself at a precarious angle and with as much enthusiasm as he could muster shouted, "Here we go, hold on to your hat." With a mighty pull he nearly jacked out of the raft. His oars couldn't reach the water.

Horace climbed out, removed his sneakers, rolled up his pants legs, waded into the water and tugged her end of the raft free from the bottom where he feared she might take root. This got them afloat enough that he could climb aboard.

Once they were underway they zig-zagged back and forth in small spurts for what seemed like an eternity. At one point she said, "My, this fresh air certainly does whet one's appetite. I can hardly wait until we reach the park."

Finally they bobbed beyond the dock where the raft had been moored and Horace's heart sank. The park seemed an insurmountable distance. At that same moment they were both startled when a sleek powerboat shot around a knoll and headed straight toward them. The pilot of the boat had obviously been as startled as they were and to avoid a collision, he made a sharp turn back into open water.

Horace watched in wonder as waves of considerable size, created by the wake of the boat, headed in their direction. His realization that this was going to be a tricky situation came almost too late as he hollered, "Here it comes Mrs. Snowberry. Hang on tight."

The first wall of water lifted Mrs. Snowberry's end of the raft into the air, then set her down with a resounding smack as Horace's end went air borne. This allowed the second wave to wash completely over Mrs. Snowberry. With a shriek she attempted to rise, and fell with force against the side of the raft. When the third wave hit, it shoved them back as far as the dock and they both flipped into the water.

Horace surfaced in a panic to locate his passenger and was relieved to see her bright yellow cone shape mucking ashore in knee-deep water. He noted that the pyramid hat, though taking a slight list to starboard was still intact. At least she hadn't lost her hairpiece again.

As he retrieved the raft, the picnic basket and a sneaker that floated by with a pickled quail egg in it, he wondered with gloom what her reactions to this catastrophe would be. Suffice it to say, he was relieved to see her already ensconced in his car.

Trying to lighten the mood Horace made the happy remark of "Well, that was a refreshing dip," which was met with stony silence. The ride home gave him insight into the meager joy of life in an ice bucket.

Faced again with the problem of her removal once they reached her house, he was blessed by a second visit from lady luck. He had hurried around the car to assist Mrs. Snowberry when she shook her head in what he presumed was disgust. This action loosened a minnow from beneath the brim of her hat and it landed on her bare leg. Once again, her involuntary orbit into space occurred as he opened the car door and out she sailed once again.

His hope for at least a tad of understanding on her part was for naught. His abject apologies fell like a handful of glass balls breaking against her closing door.

Chapter 12

WITH THE ARRIVAL OF FAMILY vacationers, the summer days of lakeside picnics, boating and barbecues gave the community more the appearance of a resort than a haven for easing through the golden years unimpeded.

The active and noisy grandchild-laden activities of the day mellowed out like toasted marshmallows when the water became streaked with moonlight. Eventually, the quiet conversation around dying fireside embers along the shore ended another perfect day.

Sometimes from his deck at night Horace could hear the muted sounds of laughter and conversation from the beach below. It often led him to wonder at the powers to be that had led him to settle here.

His mother had returned from her world cruise and wanting to know all about it he invited her to dinner one evening. She echoed his own sentiments when she went on to say that she believed he had found the perfect spot and seemed to take real pleasure from his surroundings and the friends he'd made. Then out came the fiddle and her favorite tune of "I do wish though that you could find some woman who..."

"Mother," he interrupted her. "I'm not yet ready to get involved again".

With visible effort she tucked her lecture back into her 'pending' file and commented on the dinner they'd just finished. "That fish was marvelous. Did you catch it here in the lake?"

"Heaven's no. I know nothing about fishing."

"Well, your father certainly loved it. He'd close the office and hang a sign on the door."

One day during one of his frequent visits to Amanda's office, she had revealed that fishing was one of her favorite things to do, and her husband-to-be allowed her to go with him on special occasions. She had also mentioned that according to legend there was a monster fish hiding in the lake that occasionally made an appearance. The next day he had himself outfitted with an assortment of piscatorial gear, most of which he knew nothing about.

Horace almost gave up after he became tired of the several painful fish hook extractions he'd had to make, as well as the cutting away of yards of line in which he had become entangled, but he finally got the hang of it and began to enjoy it.

However, his incursion onto and into the lake with Mrs. Snowberry, had spawned an unwillingness on his part to share the joy of his small craft with friends, so he always went alone.

The only person he could think of that he'd like to join him was Amanda. When he told her of all the equipment he'd bought, she, with a warm smile said, "Well, maybe someday we could go together. I think that would be fun."

That suggestion pleased him so much he spent extra hours learning all he could about the sport.

For every hang-up that needs to be thawed there's always a bag of hot air lurking in the wings. In Horace's case it came in the form of a pool table wager with Norbert Balmer, the guy who got bombed by the osprey. The two of them had arrived early one Tuesday night for the usual pool game and he sensed that he'd been lined up in the cross hairs of Norbert's gun sights as though he was an enemy ammunition dump.

"Bet'cha a cruise on that yacht of yours I can blast you into oblivion on our first game." Norbert had challenged.

"You're on. Should you win, I'll throw in the beer and sandwiches."

To no one's surprise, Horace's included, he lost, but his biggest concern was how he would stand a full day of the fellow. Norbert, as everyone agreed was a veritable whirling dervish of nervous energy. He came complete with rapier quick retorts and the ability to talk non-stop which had made him an A-one fund raiser. He was like a gnat that people dodged by sending in their larger than asked for donations ahead of time in order to avoid him.

His wife was seldom seen and never attended any of the social functions. His only reference to her came when anyone mentioned his still slender, boyish figure. "Owe it to my wife's cooking. Can't eat the gol-darn stuff," he'd reply.

At the pool table he became transformed into an eerie and silent, lean mean machine as his crew cut head bobbed after his opponent. These actions led Horace to remark to Teenut that he always felt like a bi-plane being stalked by the Stealth Bomber. Therefore he was relieved when he saw Norbert coming down the pier the next day with a casting rod and reel.

"Hey Norbert, I had no idea you fished. You don't strike me as the kind of guy who could stand still long enough to cast a line."

"Hooo, I love this stuff. Takes all the kinks out. Yes sir, give me the solitude of a lake, a boat, a fishing pole and I'm in heaven."

Horace felt perhaps a reevaluation of the man was in order except that by the time he had the gear loaded in his raft, Norbert had paid a visit to three other parties preparing to venture forth, traded off some bait for a couple of rubber worms, and collected thirty-five dollars toward a fund raiser.

Cast fishing wasn't a pastime that interfered with his gift of gab and the only time he wasn't in motion or talking either to Horace, or persons who passed by on their way to quieter spots, was when he swallowed bits of the lunch Horace had provided. This trip did however, go a long way toward melting Horace's reticence toward inviting some of his friends to share his small craft.

Throcky and her willowy niece were among his first guests, and this had not only been a delight but had given his libido a good jump start when the willowy one had dived past him in her bikini and he'd helped her climb back into the raft. The excursion with Zack and Ladenia had included her laughter at Zack's discomfort when she asked him to guess how much lake water he was replacing. He was so piqued he scooted up onto the side too fast and fell overboard.

Horace's favorite companion however, became Teenut who had less interest in fishing than he'd had, but went along anyway. He spent his time sprawled in the front end of the craft engrossed in a book or just enjoying the scenery.

On their first trip out Horace had opened his tackle box and dangled an all to real looking minnow in front of him. Teenut sat bolt upright. "My gawd man, that's not lunch is it?"

"It is. I thought we'd dine on this rare specimen, or if you prefer, we have imitation pork rind and bass bugs."

Burying himself in his book again he grumbled, "You told me you weren't a serious fisherman."

"I'm not, but as long as I had to buy so much equipment I figured I might as well look the part. Anyway, we just might catch the *big one* that's supposed to be lurking around out here."

"Hah, if you're referring to that monster fish, he hasn't been seen in 10 years."

One day when Horace and Teenut had gone out in the raft Teenut said, "Know what I like most about our excursions? I don't have to come up with some sort of intelligent conversation to astound you with."

"I'm taking that as a compliment, and the same to you."

"You know what I mean. As I see it, the two of us have reached that plateau of contentment attainable only by men."

"Correct," Horace agreed. "How many women do you know would put up with no conversation?"

"None." Teenut stated.

One late afternoon, the two men decided they'd had enough of communing with nature for one day and were headed for shore when Horace's pole bent almost double. With irritation he grumbled, "What now!"

The next thing he knew He'd slammed into Teenut and almost knocked him out of the raftt. "I think something caught us," he hollered.

As startled as Horace was, Teenut asked, "What did we run into?"

"We didn't run into anything, but whatever it is has hold of my line. I'll pull it in this direction and you get the net." At that moment a huge fish broke water standing on its tail and cavorting violently in at attempt to free itself.

After what seemed like an eternity the two men were able to drag their catch into the raft.

"That," said a breathless Teenut is the biggest large mouthed bass I've ever seen."

"How do you know what it is?" Horace asked.

"I do read. Besides, I've done some angling in my time and I can tell from the marks. See that yellow stomach with a black stripe running from cheek to tail? That's how you tell. Anything else you want to know?"

"He's right," said a stranger from another boat. "It's been ten years since anyone got a nibble on that one."

Horace and Teenut had been so busy landing their fish they hadn't realized they were now surrounded by other boats. Shaking his head, Teenut said "I assume that being a true sportsman, your intention is to return this poor creature from whence he came and allow him to live out his remaining years in peace and quiet, as you and I are doing."

"Wrong. My intention is to take this poor creature home where he will spend his golden day in an honored spot above my mantle."

A crowd of beachgoers who had noticed their commotion had gathered at the shore. As Horace held the large fish up for everyone to see he became aware that his shirt was being yanked on by someone's scruffy underfed grandchild who'd waded out to their boat.. "My grandma was watching you through binoculars and called the paper. They're coming to take your picture," he shouted.

The kid had been right. Soon a reporter and photographer from the Bee Line, purveyor of local news, misspelled words and misplaced captions, spent the next half hour doing an interview and taking pictures of Horace and Teenut.

"When do you think this will make the paper?" Horace asked the exuberant young girl reporter.

"This is big news. That fish is a legend around here. My boss told me that fish hasn't even been seen in over a decade, so he's going to run it on tomorrow's front page."

Turning to a grinning Teenut, Horace said, "This calls for a party. What say we throw a sunrise breakfast at my place tomorrow to celebrate our fame. We'll time it to coincide with the delivery of the paper."

"Sounds good to me. I can flip flapjacks behind my back," Teenut said with a grin.

That evening, his call to several of their friends generated a sense of excitement and all had agreed to come. When the paper did arrive Horace controlled his desire to sneak a peek. Instead, as everyone gathered around, he unfolded the paper which he'd tucked against his chest. There on the front page was the picture of a leering Teenut and Horace, clutching their big fish. The headline above it, which brought silence to their friends boldly trumpeted, 'TWO SEX OFFENDERS APPREHENDED."

The only sound made was when Delfinnia Coffer said in her squeaky voice, "I didn't know you could molest a fish."

The demanded retraction appeared the next day as promised. On page seven was a picture of two scruffy gents identified as resident of the retirement community of Upson Downes. The headline above their picture read simply "CATCH OF THE DECAYED."

Chapter 13

IT TOOK THE PARTICIPANTS OF the fishing fiasco, which of course the whole community had been privy to, awhile to recover. Horace immersed himself in the healing powers of sculpting and this was a perfect morning to work in his studio. The sun hadn't yet burnt off the wisps of morning fog entangled in the tree branches and the muted sounds of early morning activity at the lake were pleasant and not intrusive.

Having forgotten to put his phone on message, it rang as he stepped back to appraise the deer he had been working on. By winter time he hoped to be able to place it in his garden. The ring somehow had a discordant sound to it. The only person he knew who could elicit a sound like that from a telephone was his mother, but she was out of town and he seriously doubted her ability exceeded local calls. To stop the infernal ringing he picked it up, and was greeted by the unmistakable voice of Ladenia Blossom.

"Binky? What do you know about plumbing."

Still reluctant to back out of his artistic mood he asked in a vague tone, "Whose?"

"Mine. There was a small drip in the kitchen faucet and I figured it only needed a new washer. I loosened it to have a look and swoosh! I now have a small geyser."

"If you'll look under the sink there's a valve there where you can turn off the water."

"C'mon Binky, give me a break. Remember I had a husband who manufactured plumbing parts. Three things he made sure I knew how to do were, change a flat tire, balance my own checkbook and change a washer." I thought I'd conquered all three, but I've obviously failed the 'change a washer' test. I've tried every valve under the sink. Zack's not home and the plumber can't come until late today or maybe tomorrow morning. I don't know what to do."

Horace, who had always been a sucker for any damsel in distress said, "You keep your finger in the dyke and I'll be there soon as I get cleaned up."

"Oh Binky, I'm sorry. I can tell you're busy. What are you doing?"

"I'm working on a deer."

"Anybody I know?"

"No, but come winter, I hope to have her in my garden."

"Oooo!, Good way to catch cold," she said.

"Here, here. I'll be there in twenty minutes."

Twenty minutes later Horace tossed his tool chest on the car seat and backed out of the driveway. To his shock he almost sideswiped Teenut who was jogging by."

"Sorry, old man," he said as he slammed on the brakes. "Care for a lift?"

"Don't mind if I do," Teenut said with a gasp.

Horace started to move the toolbox, but Teenut jumped up on it and sat down. "See better from up here," he said with a laugh.

Horace marveled again at his friend's magnificent head of red hair. As they coasted down the hill Horace asked, "Say, Teenut, you ever do any plumbing?

With a chuckle he said, "Oh, I've taken care of a few drips in my time."

For some reason Teenut's humor always took him by surprise and he went on to describe Ladenia's problem. "I feel totally inadequate," Horace told him. "I think the closest I've ever come to plumbing is changing a washer in the garden hose."

"I'm not sure I'd recognize a washer, but if you need company doin' nothin', I'm your man."

Ladenia was tickled pink to have not one, but two rescuers. On entering the kitchen it was obvious she did have a problem. Water was gushing through the many towels she had wrapped around the faucet.

Horace got down on his hands and knees and examined and tried every lever under the sink, but the best he came up with was a couple of un-professional grunts. "What do all those grunts mean? Are you in the throes of some sort of gastric problem?" she asked.

"No," he hollered back. "I'm just checking to make sure we haven't missed something."

Snapping him on the bottom with a dishtowel she said, "If you don't get you rear end out of the air I'll turn *your* handle. Then we'll really have a leak."

Knowing Ladenia was a woman of her words he stood up and asked, "Where's the outside turn-off valve?" he asked.

With a casual wave of her hand Ladenia said, "Oh, under the house somewhere. I think the opening is in the garage."

Horace's elation at this golden question dissolved rapidly, but Teenut struck first. "I'm allergic to crawl spaces. Got bit by a spider once."

No way could Horace dodge the benevolent smiles being bestowed on him by Ladenia and Teenut. With a frown of resignation he grumbled, "Okay, lead the way"

"Ugh! here I go," said Horace as he opened the trap door. He shone his light here and there in hopes of finding the valve close at hand. "Yikes, there's a zoo under here," Horace said. Reaching beyond a copious nest of about to be creepy-crawlies whose guardian's beady eyes were following him with a last supper sort of look he turned the only valve he found and hollered, "That better be it, 'cause I'm out of here."

Teenut hollered "You did good little buddy. You found the right one."

Back inside Horace was gratified to see Teenut was busy replacing the faucet. When he was through he patted it softly and said, "There you go Baby, all fixed."

"What's that?" Horace asked, pointing to a small screw still on the counter.

"You would have to ask. I don't know, it came off the handle but it's too tiny to get back in and since the faucet stays on without I'm not going to worry."

Ladenia had just returned from taking the wet towels to the laundry room and Horace said, "Well, there you are my dear. This should hold you 'til the plumber gets here."

She said with consternation, "Aren't you going to turn the water back on? I don't want to be all day without it"

Teenut was looking down his nose at Horace said, with a benevolent smile, "Too bad. This is what happens when you're so talented."

Somehow the joy of this day had completely disappeared as far as Horace was concerned, as he prepared to once more grope his way past the predators lurking beneath the house. With caution he reached around a thriving pack of about-to-be arachnids in their gossamer blankets and twisted every handle he could lay his hands on. His exit from the crawl space coincided with a loud shriek. His race to the kitchen revealed a sight he would look back on for years to come, as not only unique, but enlightening.

The faucet lay in the sink and beside it, rigid with astonishment was a wide-eyed, dripping and bald Teenut who had apparently bent over the fixture at the precise moment Horace had turned on the water.

Ladenia's equally startled gaze vacillated between the gentleman in question and the ceiling. His magnificent red hair was now impaled there at the end of a stream of water that erupted from the kitchen faucet with the unbridled majesty of "Old Faithful."

At that moment the doorbell rang and Ladenia tore herself away from this bizarre scene to answer it. She returned with the plumber who was explaining he'd been called to another emergency in the neighborhood, so he figured he might as well take care of her at the same time.

As though the situation in to which he had walked was nothing out of the ordinary, including the object impaled on the ceiling he, without hesitation, tried everything under the sink and announced as though we should have known. "There's your culprit. This turn off valve needs to be replaced. It doesn't work at all."

In the silence in which the three of them were still bogged down, this small energetic icon of efficiency, chattered away in plumberese as though everyone knew what he was talking about. He then went to the crawlspace, extinguished the blast of water and hurried back to the kitchen. This time lapse allowed Teenut's soggy 'rug to plop onto the counter like a piece of fresh liver.

The plumber then quickly replaced the defunct valve, reattached the faucet with the small screw intact, returned to the crawl space, turned on the water and still babbling, came back to the kitchen, made out his bill and said, "You can mail the check. Oh by the way, I took the liberty of killing a very large spider and its soon to be family under the house. I don't like to do that to any of God's creatures, but that was a really mean one."

Horace visibly paled at this news, but his biggest concern was Teenut and what he could do to ease his embarrassment.

Soggy hairpiece reattached he stood and stared at the two of them in abject misery. In a barely audible voice he said, "I guess you could say I blew my top."

Shaking her head as she laughed softly in relief Ladenia said, "The same thing happened to my late husband, but it was Mrs. Snowberry's plumbing he was tending. His hairpiece fell into the garbage disposal, and she became so excited at seeing him in the nude she turned the disposal on."

We all had a good laugh at that one. Then Ladenia walked over to Teenut and gave him a big hug. "I have to tell you honey, I love bald men almost as much as I love secrets and this is one secret I'll cherish forever."

Chapter 14

THE HANDSOME POSTER, COMPLETE WITH pictures, which had appeared on an easel in the entry to the clubhouse, had become the topic of excited conversation.

The professional placard heralded the news that Dora Thudpucker and her husband Theophilus, new to the community and with broad experience in the theater, had offered to lend their expertise toward a thespian endeavor to be participated in by the residents. "*Come one, come all. There will be a task for everyone,*" beckoned the eye-catching caption.

"Who the heck are the Thudpuckers?" asked Ladenia. "And if we *come one-come all* as the notice says, who will be left to *come see* the play?"

"I met the lady at coffee and cookie hour the other morning," Alvina said. "In the short time they have been here, her observations of the residents tell her we are ripe for an endeavor like they've proposed."

With a snort Ladenia said, "I for one would like to know what proposal I'd be endeavoring before I expose my lack of talent. I must say though it's the most exciting thing that's come along since Horace and Teenut were exposed as the perverts of Upson Downes."

With a cocky toss of her head Throcky said, "I'll have you know I once played Peter Pan."

Horace, eyeing her with curiosity was about to make a remark when she stopped him. "I know exactly what you're thinking, Binky. Wow, block and tackle to get her into the air."

"I haven't said a word," he countered in self defense.

"Maybe not, but your look said it all. You must remember that the shape of me to come wasn't as yet a reality."

Horace in turn succumbed to the cleansing aspect of tell all and admitted, "My only stint on the boards was during my kindergarten days when I played a mouse in the Pied Piper of Hamelin."

Choking on her drink Ladenia said, "Why is it so easy to picture you as a rodent."

"Because of your devious mind," Horace countered. "The only thing I really remember about it was that my mother yanked me off stage by my tail when I insisted on joining the cats in their dance number. It came off in her hand and made her so mad she hit me with it."

Zack, having just joined the conversation said, "My claim to stardom came in high school when I was Puck in A Midsummer Night's Dream. I got too fancy prancing around in the underbrush until I tripped and fell off the stage into a kettle drum. Made a big hit---well, at least a big noise."

With a burst of laughter Ladenia said, "We have a tailless rodent, and an oversize fairy flitting into a kettle drum and no doubt sounding like the end of the 1812 Overture. How could Dora Thudpucker have known she would be farming a veritable garden of latent talent?"

Everyone seemed to be in agreement that the Thudpuckers would be hard put to find enough participants. However, in a quieter moment, the candle of possibility was lit in each one of them, that perhaps under the tutelage of someone as talented as Dora Thudpucker, their dormant abilities could come to fruition.

When the first meeting of would-be Thespians was announced, Horace had a tug of war with his conscience. "If I was given a part say, like the suave sophisticated roles Cary Grant used to play, I could make a dent in theater annals as a rising star," he told himself.

On the day of the meeting he had to push his way into the room. Everyone he knew was there including Teenut, who had been the most vocal in denial that anything like this could arouse his interest.

With a loud clap of hands a beaming Mrs. Thudpucker, rose, took center stage and asked for silence. She was a short, large-boned woman with bleak features. Heavy make-up on her dark piercing eyes did nothing to soften her image. Ebony tresses hung down either side of her stark white face in knife like precision, interrupted only by a slash of bright red lipstick.

Draped in a flowing black, floor length garment with white inner-lined sleeves she did, in spite of her diminutive size, present an impressive figure. Clearly, this was a woman who inspired and got attention. Visibly exhilarated by the turnout, her stentorian voice froze the group in their places.

"Welcome." She bellowed in her powerful voice. "We are overwhelmed by your generous response." In a broad gesture clearly meant to produce the other half of the "We", she demanded, "Theo! Where are you?"

A small thin man peeked a balding head fringed with white, from behind the protrusion that was his wife. Clad in faded blue overalls, blue and white plaid shirt, bare feet tucked into blue buckle-on sandals he twitched his fingers and smiled in a shy greeting.

Once more in charge, Mrs. Thudpucker, or Dora as she beseeched us to call her said, "Your response has overwhelmed us and I have a confession to make. Theo and I decided years ago that should we ever be blessed with such a large turnout we would produce not one, but two plays, so that everyone has a chance."

This news which Horace felt would do nothing toward easing Ladenia's concern of *if everyone is in the play who would come see it* was met with a round of applause and kindled the growing excitement as each one's hidden talents began to ooze beneath their closed doors.

Dora put up her hand to still the chatter which had begun to sound like a bevy of chipmunks set free in a forest of oaks, and said in an excited voice, "The two plays we decided on are, first, "Romeo and Juliet, which of course we all know and love. The second is a favorite of mine and will be a true challenge, but seeing this enthusiastic crowd, I have no doubt we will rise to that challenge together and in triumph."

With arm upraised as her hand clutched the air in an attempt to tether the rise that was in danger of ballooning out of control, she continued. "The second play is the lesser known, but powerful Scandinavian Volsunga Saga on which Wagner later based his beloved *Ring of* The Nibelungs."

In an incredulous voice Ladenia asked, "Were doing an opera? Most of us can't carry a tune in a hand basket."

With a toss of her head Dora said in a strangled voice, "No, no, dear, nothing so worldly." With a stricken look as she stretched out her arms and opened her hands as though in receipt of manna from heaven, she enunciated in a dramatic whisper, "This will be done in beautiful twelfth century prose."

For those who weren't still looking heavenward in anticipation of our free delivery of manna, this explanation was about as clear as a mud puddle on a rainy day.

Horace had trouble picturing Dora as demure Juliet, but after her announcement about the Volsunga Saga, he had no trouble picturing her as a Valkyrie.

As if in anticipation of our concerns that if everyone participated there would be no one left to see the plays, she said, "I have already obtained permission from the board to open up our performances to the towns-people. In fact, the board has offered to foot the bill for the publicity."

This spawned many "Ohs" and "Ahs" in Phil Coffer's direction as being the knight in shining armor who had untied the purse strings.

She went on to assure the audience that "Everyone will have a part," although, she did stress that part didn't always refer to an acting role. Then she explained. "There are sets to build, costumes to sew and a myriad of other behind the scenes tasks that are as important, if not more so, than acting. My husband Theo---Theo! where are you? Theo will be in charge of the work crews. Those of you interested in that aspect, meet with him in the next room"

Theo, who didn't look like he wanted to be in charge of anything, shuffled off to his designated post with several people shuffling behind him.

"Now," said Dora to her adoring audience, "Those who would like to act there are sheets from a variety of plays. Pick one you like, take it home to rehearse, and meet here with me tomorrow morning at ten."

Horace felt slightly deflated that his launch into the world of the theater had to wait a day, but was pleased when he found many roles he felt could showcase his smoldering talent.

The announcement the next day that Horace had been chosen to play Romeo, left him in a bag of mixed emotions, and in all modesty, he said to Zack, "That's a shocker. I was afraid I'd over-emoted."

Zack, always the leveler said in his stony voice, "If I'd had a can labeled ham, I would have stuffed you in it."

Horace was delighted when the role of Juliet was given to Alvina. While Alvina's sweet demeanor fit the bill character-wise, her frail voice presented a problem. Dora came to the rescue and proceeded to stuff a microphone down the cleavage of Alvina's dress.

As in most worthy endeavors where people with a united cause pull together in a concerted effort, the days flew by. Under the keen eye of Dora's husband, Theophilus, whose ability and creativity attained amazing results once he was on his own, costumes were being made, make-up classes were held, lighting installed, and sets were built and painted.

However after several days, this Christmas like atmosphere started to erode into huffs, tantrums and foot stamping by several individuals who felt their artistic abilities were not being recognized. The announcement that heralded the actual dates of the shows came in the nick of time. On that day Norbert Balmer, who hadn't realized Mrs. Snowberry was anywhere in the area was doing a credible imitation of her as a Brynhild when he was beaned on the head by her purse to which she was attached. He had to be helped off the ship.

Zack, whose barrel-chested figure had gained him the part of Sigurd to Mrs. Snowberry's Brynhild in the Volsunga Saga was pacing back and forth as he memorized his lines. Horace noted that Zack had mastered a hefty swagger, a mannerism he'd taken to doing off stage until Ladenia told him in no uncertain terms, "If you don't cut that out, I'll sink your barge in the nearest fjord---with you on it.'

Dora's only comment as she beamed in a benevolent manner through these weird antics was, "Now you're behaving like real troupers."

It was never determined whether it was out of a real appreciation for live theater, or out of a morbid sense of curiosity that the townspeople responded so generously, but they did. Both performances were sold out.

Horace was pleased when each participant was offered two free tickets to the shows. He hurried to the office to give one to Amanda. To his pleasured surprise she gave him a hug as she said, "Oh Horace, I'm so proud of you."

Delighted, he had turned to leave when her fiancé walked in and he reluctantly offered him the other ticket.

Horace sensed a lot of confusion among cast members, and the people backstage who had to shift sets back and forth and even he kept reminding himself that Romeo and Juliet was on Friday night and Volsunga Saga was on Saturday.

On Friday night, Horace had arrived early for his performance in Romeo and Juliet, and was in such a nervous state he feared life threatening illness was imminent. “Oh why did I ever give those tickets to Amanda and her fiancé,” he kept lamenting over and over.

Both Thudpuckers were very supportive and assured him the feelings he was agonizing over would soon disappear. “Once you are on stage, those butterflies will leave and go back wherever they came from.”

Horace sincerely wished the butterflies would take him with them. It had seemed to him that his wife had always taken an inordinate amount of time putting on panty hose and as he struggled to get into his before donning his breeches, he was interrupted by Ladenia’s rap on the door. “Hoo hoo, I’m here to do make-----what in the world are you doing”

Horace gave her a threatening look and grimaced, “Only a woman could have thought up such a torture. These blasted things are hard enough to get on as it is, and then before you’re even done they start sagging around your ankles like alligator skin.”

With a laugh she said, “Your problem Binky is, you don’t have a bottom to hang them on.”

Horace found that the Thudpuckers had been right. Once he was on stage his butterflies disappeared and in fact his confidence was such that when Alvina, who had been doing so well as Juliet failed to appear for their balcony scene he took it in stride. “I’ll bet her nervousness got to her. I’ll just give her a little more time.” He climbed higher up the ladder with what he considered unusual grace and in an understated touch of mounting passion he adlibbed, “Juliet, oh Juliet, tis’ I Romeo, your true love.”

What appeared next was not the sweet demure Juliet but the behemoth figure of Mrs. Snowberry as Brynjhild, complete with Valkyrian regalia, including spear. Beating her more than ample bosom with her fist she roared, "I take wolves to suck."

Horace, nearly startled out of his senses and paralyzed by this declaration, bleated, "But Mrs. Snowberry, it's Friday. You don't come on until tomorrow night."

With an inadvertent push against the balcony he sent the ladder on which he was standing, backward into the ropes that controlled the curtain. This paraphernalia came crashing down as the audience erupted in gales of laughter, whistles and wild cheers. "Whoever said, "The show must go on," hadn't met up with this troupe.

No one moved, not even the thunderstruck Thudpuckers.

The audience, assuming the play was over with this comedic ending, streamed out still laughing amidst remarks of "Funniest dang thing I ever saw."

In true professional manner and to their credit, Dora and Theo, with no mention of any names, gathered what was left of their pride and the cast. In a resounding voice Dora announced, "The Volsunga Saga will go on tomorrow night as scheduled." With that she swept out of the room as Theo, caught up in her wake swept rapidly behind her.

The municipality that surrounded Upson Downes was no exception to that old saying *news travels fast in small towns.* Assuming they were to be treated to another hilarious performance, an overflow crowd showed up the next night.

Three hours later when the ponderous play plodded to its demise, those members of the audience still in attendance had to be awakened.

A few weeks later, when the Thudpuckers disappeared from the scene, Horace said in their defense, "They are after all, snowbirds and being it was nearing that time of year, they had probably gone south a little early to avoid the rush."

When the For Sale sign appeared on their lawn, everyone said, "Well, I'm not surprised."

Chapter 15

As THE FIELDS OF SUMMER wheat turned to gold, and the cool winds of autumn sent bright colored leaves scurrying so too did the social scene in Upson Downes take on a different hue. The activities agenda became cozier and a tad more formal.

Horace's *Chef de Cuisine* hat, though somewhat worse for wear, had withstood the rigors of his modest culinary contribution of dinners on the grill. Kind folks had told him that his Caesar Salads were morsels to die for, an accomplishment he felt he owed to the perseverance of his former wife. She hated making salads and relegated that duty to him.

Frankly he was happy to tuck his barbecue tools into the confines of the bottom drawer until next year. Not that he would ever underestimate the sight and smell of a beautiful roast as it undulated slowly on the spit of his indoor grill, but it seemed that people leaned more toward the tried and true traditional foods of hearty stews, heavy simmering soups and slow roasted meat.

To plan meals beyond the few talents he possessed was something he didn't do and he remarked on this fact to Zack one day as they shivered in a duck blind alongside the lake. It was their hope that dinner would soon fly by. Ladenia had told them that "If you bring it I'll cook it."

"I sure remember your one and only venture into preparing dinner sans the grill. That was a real blast and I hadn't had so much fun since I was a kid," Zack told him.

Horace had to laugh. "Those cheese rolls I made to go with my cucumber soup hatched into darn good bowling balls, though they didn't hold a candle to the bread sticks I made once. Could've used those as bats. I took some up to my mother, who gave them to her housekeeper, who put them out for the birds."

"Well, at least somebody got some good out of them," remarked Zack.

"Oh no, because Mr. Littlebury ran over one with the mower and busted a blade."

At that moment their chances of actual participation in a roast duck dinner improved one hundred percent as Zack up and nailed a beauty. The next morning as Horace reflected on the wonderful dinner of the night before, his phone rang.

"Bink?" breathed Drusilla Sebastian in her husky voice. "I've decided to give a Thanksgiving dinner party and I need a co-host. You know, someone to fill in for the little man."

Warily, Horace asked, "What do you mean by fill in for the little man?"

"You know, ply the throng with drinks, serve the peanuts, carve the turkey, help with the dishes, that sort of thing."

"Oh, right you are. Sounds good, but I'd best warn you. Other that shoving the turkey into the oven and closing the door, that's as far as my expertise goes."

"Don't worry," she assured him. "I have this wonderful recipe my mother has used for years. You encase the bird in clay and it cooks in its own juice. It has an incredible flavor and is so easy to do."

Horace, was actually relieved to hear that Drusilla actually had a mother. "Sounds good, when do we start this project?"

Her voice became husky again as she said, "I knew I could count on you. Come over tomorrow morning at ten and we'll line up our ducks. It's better to be prepared early."

After he hung up Horace began to have an uneasy feeling about the whole thing. "What am I getting into? I hardly know this woman," he mused to himself.

His first encounter with her had occurred when, with a frantic ring of a bicycle bell and a shout of "Look out, no brakes," she had shot between Zack and Horace as they were going to their cars after a golf game. She had run smack dab into a curb and flown over the handlebars into a hedge. They of course had hurried to her assistance.

She had brushed them aside saying, "Other than a few twigs lodged in some uncomfortable places, I seem to have all my parts; at least the important ones."

Introductions were made and when it was learned she was a newcomer, Horace said, "I'd be very pleased if you'd come to dinner at the club tonight as my guest."

She had accepted with delight and started to get back on her bike when Zack called out in concern, "I hope you're not going to ride with no brakes. That's much too dangerous."

With a wave of her hand she said, "Not to worry, It's all up hill from here."

With a shake of his head Horace said, "What a remarkable woman. Odd, but remarkable."

While she had seemed an oddity to Horace she was more so to the women at the dinner that night. Many of the ladies were overwhelmed by her quick no-nonsense manner and underwhelmed by her sometimes rowdy humor. Her chameleon like demeanor could change from tough to enticingly feminine in the twitch of an eye, and it made them nervous. "She's dangerous," one skittish female was heard to mutter.

After Drusilla had become a regular, her open, friendly and outspoken manner, and the innocent questioning look that followed her remarks, often left a person with the uneasy feeling that she was enjoying some private bit of merriment at their expense.

Ladenia, with that illusive feminine intuition so foreign to men, sensed that underneath Drusilla's candid manner lay an intelligent and sophisticated woman of the world, and it was her approval of the lady that became the catalyst for her acceptance by others.

Drusilla's blond tresses, which one wag claimed showed signs of having been several other colors, were worn in soft waves around the perfect proportions of her oval face and drawn to the back in a pony tail that cascaded half-way down her knockout figure.

Horace had discovered one night as they were dancing, that her large, heavily lashed, almond shaped eyes, made him want to raise the lids farther and peek inside. Her legs, which men turned to marvel at, caused women to hurry home and dig out their slacks to hide their own imperfections.

Another odd thing was her occasional attire of knickers with matching blouses in striking colors and fabrics. This of course caused more than a few raise eyebrows and the word *bizarre* was hissed among the women, while the preferred expression in men's circles was, *exotic,* accompanied by a secretive smile and far-away look.

She had on occasion referred to *my husband* the artist, whom no one had ever seen. It was odd that everyone, and that included outspoken Ladenia, had been too polite to ask if the reference was to the living or the dead.

Another thing the ladies harrumphed about was Drusilla's live in maid. This was a luxury not indulged in by anyone else in the community. All these things were running through Horace's mind when he rang her doorbell.

The door was opened by a middle-aged lady with a scrubbed face, her brownish graying hair was braided around her head like a halo.

"Mr. Bink?"

"Yes, I'm here to---"

"I know why you're here. Follow me please.

Horace tailed after the stout figure and noted she wore no fancy uniform. A kitchen apron over a plain frock, support hose and sensible shoes made up the rest of her attire.

She stepped aside as she opened the door and he found to his astonishment he'd been ushered into Drusilla's boudoir. To his further consternation, she was in a huge and rather high, four poster bed albeit swathed in a filmy cloud of pink lingerie. He was sure this had to be a mistake and said in dismay, "I beg your pardon," as he started to back out.

"For heaven's sake come on in," she said with a laugh. "I never move around much before noon. Hulda brings my coffee and morning paper in here. Have a seat."

The only thing Horace saw to sit on was a chair laden with other filmy pink things. Amused at his discomfort she patted the bed and said with a low chuckle, "Looks like this is the only place left. Come on up."

Then in that sleepy whisky voice of hers she drawled, "Don't worry, I don't get around to shifting gears 'til the cocktail hour."

Horace, feeling like an awkward schoolboy, removed his shoes and gingerly scooted up on the bed. He was immediately handed a small tray-table by Hulda on which were a croissant and a steaming cup of coffee. Her casual manner suggested that these circumstances were not unusual.

Horace sensed that this woman whose bed he was sharing was observing him with open amusement. He tried to conjure up some light conversation when he noticed a large Lapis Cabochon, surrounded by tiny diamonds on one finger. "What a beautiful and unique ring. Did you find that here in town?"

Holding her hand out in front of her she said, "Thank you, but no it isn't from around here. My husband brought it back last year from one of his many trips to the Far East."

At the mention of a husband, Horace began to feel a little easier as he said, "I've not had the pleasure of meeting your husband, in fact I don't think I've ever seen him."

"Sometimes I feel the same way. He's an artist and feels it imperative to his work to experience the people and places he paints. I used to tag along, but I'm a creature who likes a king size bed and my ice in a glass." She winked at Horace as she continued, "I told him to come home when he got good and hungry, if you get my drift."

Horace did get the drift but to keep from drifting to far off course he said "What can I do to help you in this venture of yours?"

Reaching over and patting his hand she said, "Our venture."

To his relief, she settled right down and he was surprised and relieved that she had actually gone so far as to make out a list. Referring to her notes she said, "I'm going to leave encasing the bird in clay in your capable hands. Let's see, oh yes, the wine. I'll leave that selection to you and by the way, how are you at making hors d'oeuvres? Most men hate it."

Once again Horace silently thanked his ex-wife. Along with salad, this was the one other thing she didn't like making, so he took over the job and out of desperation had learned some neat things to make.

Seeing an opportunity to boast a little, he said, "How about asparagus spears wrapped in roast beef, or maybe some Dijon dill shrimp? Smoked salmon is always good, as is stuffed mushrooms with crabmeat, or scallops wrapped in bacon. Of course one of my favorites is bites of chilled sherried chicken breast."

She regarded him with open amusement and a mischievous smile. "Hmm, chilled, sherried chicken breasts. I couldn't get further than tadpole titties on toast. You're on."

Much to Horace's consternation he giggled at this remark. His discomfort was further compounded by the sudden entrance into the room of an incredibly handsome fellow, whose attire indicated he was a man of the cloth.

With a delighted gasp Drusilla held both hands out to him "Father Geiger. How nice to see you again so soon. It was only last Sunday I bared my soul to you in that tiny cubicle you hang out in."

At this point Horace wished he didn't exist, but Father Geiger completely overlooked him as he took both of Drusilla's hands in his. "And tell me, what has she got you doing?" he asked, still not looking at Horace.

While Horace was trying to recover his manhood in order to give a straight answer, the good Father continued, "Beware of her charms. She can be most manipulative."

At that statement Horace surmised the padre had at some time or other occupied the position he now held. "Care to join us?" he asked.

"No thank you. I only stopped by to steal one of Hulda's croissants and thank this lovely lady for her generous gift to our orphanage fund. She's an angel, but I have to move on. I have other stops to make."

Drusilla blew him a kiss as she said, "He's always out taking tally of his flock. Old Geiger counter, his parishioners call him."

After old Geiger counter had disappeared along with his hearty chuckle and one of Hulda's croissants, the two of them got back to business and completed the plan of attack for their Thanksgiving bash. Horace arrived home feeling somewhat unglued, but more worldly wise than when he'd left. Grudgingly he had to admit, the woman intrigued him.

The invitations to their party were mailed out, a sit down dinner for sixteen was in the works and all too soon the big day arrived. Hulda had been sent off on to visit her family for the holiday. As Horace made hors d'oeuvres and slathered layers of clay on the bird, it occurred to him that filling in for the little man was becoming a full time job.

The four tables looked beautiful set with fine china, silver and crystal on subtle autumn colored linen. By the time the guests began to arrive, Drusilla and he were both quite relaxed after taste testing the different wines, and were bubbling over with infectious gaiety.

She was a big hit in her autumn colored silk knickers and matching blouse. Mrs. Snowberry, who had pursued her around like a puppy dog, at last cornered the lady and was heard to say, "My dear, what a stunning outfit. Would it be presumptuous of me to ask who your knicker maker is?"

Horace choked on his drink over the image of Mrs. Snowberry flapping around Upson Downes in a tent size replica of what Drusilla was wearing. This choking somehow caused a domino effect of bizarre proportion.

By accident Horace had bumped into Judge Gotbomb, and that triggered one of his emissions. This in turn caused a panicky exit of the people in his vicinity. As they bumped into each other, the contents of Ford Pickup's glass sloshed into Ladenias' empty one. Nervously downing this bounty in one gulp, the strong contents caused her to gasp, and in the involuntary action of raising her arm, she managed to induce Phil Coffer to stuff up his nostril a large olive on the end of a toothpick.

The two tallest men in the crowd, Father Geiger, who had come by to give the blessing, and Ford, who hadn't, rose above the disturbance. Ford had presence of mind enough to switch on the ceiling fan.

Previous to this lively incident Norbert Balmer had remarked, "That heavenly smell coming from the kitchen could activate the bomb doors on a plane at thirty thousand feet."

Drusilla, who overheard this remark, clapped her hands and called for attention. To Horace's pleasured embarrassment, she took him by the arm and said, “Thanks to this generous man you are about to experience a special treat.”

At that moment a thunderous explosion from the kitchen punctuated her announcement.

Zack in a dumbfounded voice said, “Binkbottom I didn’t know you were going to do fireworks. How clever of you.”

After an initial pause Horace cautiously crept forward, with everyone else creeping behind him. Opening the door they were stupefied to see the kitchen walls encased with dangly pieces of what look like old moss. The oven door had blown clear off the stove.

Delfinia Coffer pointed to an oddity that still clung to it and asked in her squeaky voice, “Euuw! What is that?”

Teenut bowed his head and intoned in a deep voice, “The Pope’s nose.”

Mortification eclipsed Horace like a light burning out, but Drusilla, burst into laughter. “Bink, you forgot to put vent holes in the clay.”

“Oh no,” moaned Horace. “I’ve ruined everything.”

With another burst of laughter Drusilla said “I think it’s the funniest thing I’ve ever seen.”

“But the dinner party is ruined,”

Drusilla took Horace’s arm and said gaily, “Hey this is still our party and if delivered pizza is all we can get to go with our peas and mashed potatoes, that’s what we’ll have.

It was---and they did.

Chapter 16

WHEN CLOAKED IN SNOW, WHAT slopes there were in Upson Downes lent themselves to a modest pursuit of winter sports. Using cross-country skis or snowshoes were not only popular as pastimes, but for a few they were a favorite means of transportation to social engagements. Ladenia Blossom, the only woman brave enough to hazard this mode of travel always ended up in an argument with Zack at evening's end because, although the streets were well lit, he felt someone alone on show shoes could be hard to see, and that was far to dangerous, so he insisted on driving her home.

One evening at Zack's house they had sung themselves silly and also been entertained by the piano wizardry of Mrs. Knowall, or Cookie, as we discovered her name was. She was new to our group and Horace, who hadn't seen her since the spring dance, was delighted to find out that Teenut had brought her.

Horace remembered how hard it had been to match this attractive lady he'd met at the dance, to the person who had called on the phone to ask his help with the CPR class. She was of medium height, actually, about the same as Teenut. She had a nicely rounded figure, beautiful green eyes, and lovely face framed by dark short hair in one of those casual cuts that always looked good no matter what. When she got to the piano, there wasn't a tune she didn't know, and lit with joy into any song a person might request.

Teenut had told Horace, "One day I heard her practicing on the piano at the clubhouse and was so entranced I asked her to dinner,"

With a grin Horace said, "Off listening to a piano player eh? Now I know why you keep disappearing."

Looking embarrassed, and with a big smile Teenut said in his shy way, "I'd decided to keep things on the back burner until I was sure the situation was going somewhere. Actually we're still at the hand holding stage, but I'm getting there."

All through the evening Ladenia had kept hinting that at evening's end she had a surprise for everyone, especially Zack, the worry wart. As the festivities wound down we gathered outside in anticipation of her surprise. She held up a small remote module and said, "Watch now."She pressed a button and her snowshoes were instantly outlined in tiny twinkling lights. "Shoe lights" she said proudly.

Zack was immensely impressed. "Incredible, but I still want you to call when you get home," he said as he gave her a big hug.

Teenut, who had shunned any attempts to interest him in winter sports, and had come up with a rather profound proclamation of, "I'm not walkin' anywhere on a pair of ping pong paddles or elongated chop sticks so stop askin.", had circled Ladenia with interest. With an exaggerated bow he said, "Henceforward, you shall be known as *Our lady of the footlights*."

Delighted with everyone's positive reaction, she hollered over her shoulder as she started off, "Ta-ta. See you at the races."

When Horace awoke the next morning he noticed that the world outside was wrapped in a fresh blanket of snow. Leaning on one elbow as he surveyed this beautiful sight, he thought to himself, I need a mental health day. No people and no noise except the quiet swoosh skis make when gliding across snow. The only person he could think of who would be welcome in his solitary world would be Amanda. With difficulty he put that out of his mind as he recalled her recent flurry of activities in preparation for her wedding.

Noting the road in front of his place was being plowed he decided to launch his efforts off the back slope. It had a more defined grade than the road did, but there were spaces where he'd have time to stop before he reached a rather large snow berm on the lower road.

His take off was aborted when the unmistakable squeaky voice of his nearest neighbor, Delfinnia Coffer, crackled through the cold air. "Wait for us Binky," she hollered.

"Oh no", he winced as her voice ricocheted off his head.

The physical resemblance of Delfinnia to her sister Ladenia, was where their likeness ended. Personality wise she was as mousy and subdued, as her sister was sparkly and outgoing. Her one prominent idiosyncrasy was an uncanny ability to hit the nail on the wrong end when it came to comments. Her sweetness and helplessness that stirred everyone's protective instincts often became over-shadowed by the effect of her voice on ones nervous system. It was like a fingernail scraping down a blackboard. However, her meager personality took on a third dimension with the story her husband Phil loved to tell about the time she'd gone along when he took delivery of a new hearse. She'd grown weary on the long return trip home, climbed in the back, lay down on the gurney and dragged a sheet over her.

As night approached Phil pulled up to the drive through window of a fast food restaurant. He'd ordered two burgers, two fries and two coffees, to go. The boy in the window, who was showing signs of nervousness about a double order being placed by the only visible person in a hearse, nearly lost it when Delfinnia rose up in the window and squawked, "No onions."

As these two people approached him Phil said, "Hope we're not intruding. We were going to go down the road, but the plow will be there for some time. This hill looks awfully steep. Any tips on a safe and sane approach to it?"

"Not really, I'd say the best thing is to work your way slowly back and forth so you have a chance to stop before you get to that big berm across from Mrs. Snowberry's house. If you were to get up a good head of steam and sail over that, there's no telling whose chimney you'd land in."

With a nod at their skeptical evaluation of his direction, Horace said," See you at the bottom of the garden," and shoved off. When he got to the lower road he was puzzled to see the two figures were still on the rim of the slope. When they did push off, they came straight down with Phil in the lead but not quite far enough. "Oh no," Horace said in dismay. Delfinnia's left ski was between the two of Phil's, which locked them in an unalterable position. Phil's awareness of this impediment between his feet came too late. He let out a resounding, "Aiiee" as he prepared to meet whatever fate was dishing out.

Horace could only watch in fascination as the two figures, one straight and tall like the captain of a sinking ship and the other, with arms frozen at half mast like a bird with two wounded wings, neither stopped at, nor went over the berm, but sailed neatly through it in pure cookie cutter fashion.

Horace climbed through the decorative swathe they'd carved and found them draped over Mrs. Snowberry's mailbox. Other than being in a slight state of shock and out of breath they seemed no worse for wear.

Except for distant hand waves which were never returned, Horace's only contact with Mrs. Snowberry since their fateful raft trip had been at Drusilla Sebastian's Thanksgiving party; an event almost as catastrophic. Not eager to add any more notches on her measuring pole of his character led him to suggest to the Coffers that they all mush on.

Phil, glancing over at his wife, who at the moment looked like a rag doll newly run through a wringer, said in a tottery voice, "If you don't mind, I think we'll creep home and have a go at the hot tub."

Relieved and eager to get on with his original quest of a quiet and pristine glide through the countryside by himself, he declined their kind offer to join them. As he cruised down the slight slope next to the golf course, he spied what appeared to be a flock of colorful game birds along the lakeshore. He'd never seen anything to match their odd shapes and muted sound. In excitement he cruised closer and pulled up behind a clump of bushes.

At that moment the unmistakable guffaw of Zack Finney crackled through the air with the sharpness of an ice saw. His supposed bevy of fowl turned out to be Alvina and Jepson Gotbomb, Zack and Ladenia and Colonel Pignut, a newcomer in the community. They had all met up quite by accident while pursuing individual athletic pursuits. They were huddled around a meager fire in one of the pits on the beach.

The only time Horace had met the Colonel, had disaster written all over it. He'd first heard of him from Amanda. He'd walked in to her office one day as she was hanging up the phone. With a frown she'd said, "Another complaint from a resident about that new mail box on the lake road that has those huge steer horns on it. It belongs to a Colonel Pignut who recently bought the property. He's a retired rancher from Texas and hasn't built yet, but said he wanted to, as he put it, *mark his spot.* Of course that sort of thing is not allowed here and will have to be moved out of sight."

Horace's introduction to the Colonel, involved an incident of mistaken identity. He was making his way through the crowd at a recent social to-do where the Colonel, now a bona fide member of the community was in attendance. At the time of this incident Horace was enjoying a talk with Drusilla Sebastian who never failed to capture his attention. In the maze of garbled conversation he heard the unfamiliar voice of someone expounding on their prowess, bravery and skill in the matter of a two handed quick draw use of revolvers. Although not fully focused on what he was hearing, the boast of, "I tell you, my ability to get off the first bead, has discouraged many a rustler or any other brassface who was foolin' around my property," came through loud and clear.

The next claim of "By the time I was through with 'em, they knew they'd been dealt with by a man," completely eclipsed his attention of Drusilla. He had turned to see where this diatribe was coming from and had to duck in order to miss a wild arm swing by Norbert Balmer. He was deep in his own demonstration of taking on a squadron of German Messerschmitts. As a result, Horace had bumped the Colonel square in the middle of his narrative and knocked the fellow's ten-gallon hat off.

Unbeknownst to Horace, the Colonel possessed a long cascade of tired looking corkscrew curls that fell across the shoulders of his western style shirt, like day old pasta. When his hat flew off the only thing Horace saw was a mass of kinky hair and he sputtered, "I beg your pardon Madam."

The next thing Horace saw as madam turned toward him was that *she* was a *he* with a bright red face and a voice that thundered in indignation. "SIR!"

It's funny how in frozen moments of time, one can still possess the ability to take in details. In spite of his recognizance that he was in imminent danger of being emasculated, Horace's focus had become centered on the shape of the man. His powerful top half was in delicate balance on the tapered lower part, with bowed legs that seemed to start at the waist. Horace had to squelch his curiosity that would have him walking behind the fellow to see if he had a bottom. He was able to control his laughter which was good because the Colonel's face had now become outlined in purple.

Ladenia had jumped into the fray with a nervous, "Binky, I don't think you've met my new neighbor, Colonel Pignut."

With this revelation, everything popped into focus and he realized the safest route lay in a quick exit. With profound apologies he back away from the fracas and went in search of a quiet spot in which to dangle his confusion. He hadn't seen the Colonel again until now, which in his book was far too soon.

Now, thanks to Alvina, who looked like a snow bunny in a white furry outfit, this awkward moment was eased over when she said, "Binky, let me pour you some hot coffee."

Her husband Jepson struggled to his feet and said, "No no, my dear. You keep yours. I'll pour from my decanter."

From the fumes that mushroomed from the cup the judge had handed him, he wondered if it might also contain the lining of his decanter. Finding a spot on a log as far from Colonel Pignut as possible, he listened to the idle conversation of Ladenia, who was talking about the up-coming Christmas party at the club house.

"I can hardly wait," she said. "I've already decided which dress I'm going to-------what in the world is that? The disbelief in her voice brought everyone's attention to an oddity occurring out on the ice.

Jumping up the Colonel gasped, "Hot dang, he said he'd do it and he did."

Not knowing what the Colonel meant Horace asked, "Who's doing what and where?"

"It's Norbert Balmer," said Zack. "He promised Mrs. Snowberry he'd teach her to ice skate and he's doing. it."

At that moment Horace's qualms about meeting up with the lady in question were forgotten, eclipsed by the drama that was unfolding. Norbert as everyone knew, belied in appearance what his oft' told tales as a fighter pilot would presume. As he flew along the ice, his sparse stature in form fitting pants, severe military like jacket and bright red cap, gave him the appearance of an inverted exclamation mark. With one hand he propelled his pupil at a startling rate of speed across the frozen expanse, and directly toward the entranced spectators, at which point he let go of her.

We all stood spell bound as the figure of Mrs. Snowberry in a massive fur coat bore down on us. With arms outstretched and ankles turned into the ice, she looked like a superb replica of the Greek letter Pi. Zack's last minute holler of, "Stand aside," created a generous slip into which she sailed like the Viking ship from the Volsunga Saga. She weighed anchor on the only thing in her way, a sapling birch laden with snow that gave enough on impact to soften her landfall.

As the group rushed to provide what comfort they could, Horace urged, "Here, have a drink of this," and put his cup to her lips. Too late he remembered with a shudder what was in the cup and expected her to erupt like Vesuvius. He was nonplussed when, after downing the contents in one gulp she asked in a giddy voice, "Whoo! Is there any more of this good stuff around?"

In the excitement of this magnificent docking, the group had completely forgotten Norbert Balmer. There the fellow was, still on the ice with his hands across his eyes.

Horace heard a holler, or was it a bray from the Colonel, that brought Norbert to full attention and his relief on seeing Mrs. Snowberry alive and well was so great that he jerked ashore like a slinky gone berserk over the prospect of traveling down three flights of stairs unimpeded.

It wasn't long before his relaxed state matched that of his pupil who was partaking of her second cup of cheer under the solicitous tutelage of the judge.

The Colonel, who was looking Mrs. Snowberry over with a glint in his eye said, "I think I'll go fetch my car in case anyone needs a ride home."

Horace thanked the powers above for small favors. He'd been on the verge of making the same offer when a mental image flitted across his mind of Mrs. Snowberry, in her larger than life fur coat blanketing his car completely.

Another thing that crossed his mind as he watched the Colonel's continued appraisal of Mrs. Snowberry, was, that the Colonel's wife, whom he'd mentioned was away on a trip, had better hurry home.

Chapter 17

THE ANNUAL CHRISTMAS PARTY HELD at the clubhouse is the social highlight of the year and Horace had been asked to be the roving host. His duties were to welcome guests as they arrived, oversee the caterers, address any unforeseen problems and make sure that the single ladies were not left out of any of the festivities. His thoughts on this were "Ho, those tasks lie neatly within the boundary of my abilities, but how I hope my abilities don't come under Mrs. Snowberry's scrutiny."

The decoration committee had out-done themselves and the club was awash with the spirit of the season. The room was festooned with sparkling garlands, holly wreaths with red bows and what must have been hundreds of poinsettias. All this along with the lighted trees laced with dainty silver strands of beads and old-fashioned ornaments completed the picture.

During an earlier tour of the premises Horace had bumped into Cookie Knowall, who was putting final touches here and there. She was just finishing the Gotbombs table when she spotted Horace coming her way. She held up some very cute Santa Claus ornaments and with a hesitant smile whispered, "Deodorizers."

Horace nodded back his approval. Everyone agreed that she and Teenut had become the perfect happy couple. With his shy droll humor and her bubbly personality, they added fun to any gathering. At Horace's request she was going to be playing the piano during the pre-dinner hour, and a band for dancing had been hired for after dinner.

On the evening of the party and in spite of the cold night with a prediction of possible heavy snowfall before morning, the guests began to arrive in good numbers and in good humor.

Flames flickered in the two large fireplaces, one in the foyer, the other, in the dining area. Along with the soft tree lights and smell of fresh pine, it seemed as though everyone fell into the spirit of the season.

Among the early arrivals was Francis, Horace's mother. He had invited her to come as his guest, a gesture she had declined with cool politeness.

A relieved Horace had told her, "I can understand it wouldn't be any fun for you. I mean, with me having to be involved in so many things, you'd be on your own with my friends, most of whom you've never met."

Waving her hand at him she had said rather airily, "On the contrary, I'd love to come, but I would like to bring my own date."

Her date turned out to be Mr. Measles, a recent widower in town who she had described as being in need of rehabilitation. "He's taking far too long to get on with it," she complained.

Horace had met Mr. Measles at his mother's home before. The first time was at a dinner party and the second time was when he had stopped by early one morning on his way out of town and found Mr. Measles, still in robe and slippers reading the morning paper in front of the fireplace. From that he had assumed the gentleman's rehabilitation had begun in earnest.

His mother and Mr. Measles arrival coincided with that of Mrs. Snowberry. To his surprise her mink coated form gave way in gracious deference to his mother's silver-fox clad figure. Whether either fur was real or faux, was an area he didn't intend to visit.

Taking both Mrs. Snowberry's hands in his, he gave her a peck on the cheek. "Don't you look lovely, and a special merry Christmas to you." While still holding on to one of her hands he said, "Mrs. Snowberry, may I present my mother."

After a rapid double take, she blinked in disbelief, first at Horace and then at his mother as she said in a stricken voice and a look of consummate sympathy, "Oh my dear." With that she tucked her arm somewhere within the silver fox and the two of them went nodding toward the dining room together.

Mr. Measles who had been left behind said with a shake of his head, "I'll never understand women, no matter how hard I try. You look confused too. Just remember, you're not alone," and with a wink he trotted after them.

It occurred to Horace that the crowd had arrived in clusters rather than ones or two's as was their usual habit and he prevailed on Teenut and Cookie to take over greeting people at the door while he caught up with some of his other duties.

The two long buffet tables cloaked in festive covers were outlined in swags of small silver garlands entwined with tiny lights. A large crystal bowl sat in the center of each. One held punch and had an ice sculpture of a polar bear that rose out of it in dramatic splendor. The other bowl, sported a supercilious looking stuffed chicken sitting on a nest of colorful Christmas balls, and held eggnog. For the comfort of those who suspected the presence of Kool Aid in the punch bowl, or shunned dairy products in any form, a small bar had been set up in one corner.

There were the usual choices of ham, turkey and roast beef, hors d'oeuvres and salads. To Horace's delight, the orderly flow of activities allowed him to feel like a master puppeteer pulling the right strings at the right time.

At one point he noted that the eggnog bowl was at the half way mark and signaled to one of the waiters to bring another. In anticipation of its arrival he had picked up the half empty one, when he was tapped on the arm.

It was Ladenia Blossom in a knockout scarlet dress with a gold sash she'd flung casually over one shoulder. This she'd fastened to her dress with an exquisite emerald pin in the shape of an angel. It always amazed him what women could do with so little.

"Binky, I know you've met Colonel Pignut, but this is his wife Gleditsia. Isn't it wonderful that she arrived home in time for the party?"

With haste, Horace set the half-filled eggnog bowl back on a coffee table and turned to meet the Colonel's wife. Her figure, straight out of a Raphael painting, had been poured with infinite care into every inch of her rhinestone laden dress.

He managed to swallow his Adam's Apple, and was about to raise her hand to his lips, when Norbert Balmer snatched her from his grasp in a swooping dive and spun her toward the dance floor. For just a moment, he felt like he'd been stripped of the family jewels.

He turned back to the Colonel who, in his beaded jacket, shirt, pants and boots, resembled a billboard for a gambling casino and said, with utmost sincerity, "What a lucky man you are. That is a truly beautiful woman."

He was rattled out of his reverie by the sound of Ladenia clearing her throat. Her friendly smile had become laced with frost as she said icily, "Don't let us keep you from your duties…Horace."

In that instant he realized he'd let Mrs. Pignut's presence eclipse his behavior, causing him to neglect his friend. His intention to put a reassuring arm around her was rebuffed and as she stepped away from him her high heel caught in the carpet and propelled her backward where, with a small squeak, she sat down in the half full eggnog bowl he'd set there.

Both the Colonel and Horace were struck with momentary paralysis as the three of them stared at each other in disbelief. Their recovery was quick and they rushed forward to assist her.

"Better not lift her too fast. She might be stuck, in which case we'll have to carry her and the bowl out to the kitchen".

At that moment Zack, just back from a two-week stint on Naval Reserve duty, and obviously in search of Ladenia, stumbled onto this chaotic scene. Handsome and impressive in his uniform he guffawed with ill-timed humor, "There you are my dear and potted already."

At that remark, Ladenia's good nature which had shown signs of recovery at the sight of Zack, plummeted like a plane losing all power in mid flight.

Fixing the three of us with a frosty glare she hissed, "Get me out of here."

To Horace's amazement the Colonel backed away as though in fear of becoming tainted and with a tip of his hat said, "I'd better go round up that filly of mine before she bolts the barn."

Between Zack and Horace they were able to lift Ladenia's soppy form from the bowl, and much like placing an umbrella in a stand they stood her next to the heater vent. With a peck on her cheek Zack said "That'll keep you warm while I fetch your coat. Then I'll take you home to change."

As upset as Horace was by this incident, He was thankful they had been able to place her in a small alcove whose only other occupant was Ford Pickup. Sprawled in a chair, his snore would have covered the sound of a freight train passing by.

Painfully aware of Ladenia's icy silence, he was desperate to think of something to say that would bring the smile back to her face. His relief at Zack's arrival with her coat was cut short as she sailed past them toward the front door accompanied by a strange sound.

"I know she's mad as a hornet, but what is that odd sound?" asked Zack.

Horace had already figured out what it was. Putting a comforting arm around Zack's shoulder he told him, "That isn't the buzz of a hornet you hear, that noise is the sound of an overcooked omelet coming apart. We should never have stood her over the heater."

With a stricken look as he headed after Ladenia he said, "Oh my God. I wonder if I can join the Navy again? Wish me luck!"

Just then Dotson arrived on the scene. Looking at her sleeping husband she said with consternation, "Poor Ford. He's plain tuckered out. Being a school crossing guard in the cold weather makes him sleepy."

"You still helping him out?" asked Horace.

"Nah, he fired me. I used my stop sign to cream the cars of a couple of dummies that wouldn't halt for the kids. He said I was too much of a liability."

With a laugh Horace said, "You two keep up the good work. Now I'll leave you to your sleeping beauty and get back to my duties."

As he turned to leave she said, "Oh, by the way, I met your mother. She's a real hoot."

That stopped Horace in his tracks. "Did you say hoot?" he asked warily.

"Yeah you should have brought her around sooner. When I left she and Norbert had taken over the dance floor with the best exhibition of the Charleston I've ever seen, and I've seen a few."

Horace hurried back to the dining room only to find the dancing had momentarily ceased. Looking around he spied his mother in an animated conversation with Phil Coffer. With that terrible benevolent look he gets when he's nailed a burial plot sale, he was handing her a folded piece of paper from his breast pocket.

"Oh well, nothing I can do about it now. After all she is a big girl," he mused to himself.

Checking to make sure his balloon of power was still afloat and noting with satisfaction that festivities were coasting along on schedule he attended to the setting of the coffee and dessert tables and continued on his rounds.

He continued on his way and dropped into the Gotbomb's corner, He was nearly knocked over by another couple's hurried departure. That was a sure sign that the Judge's firepower was in top form and with the Judge's permission, invited Alvina to the dance floor. The musicians had taken up a slower pace under softened lights and as they glided about the floor he observed that Teenut and Cookie, looking cozy and contented, were going through some ever so graceful motions, while Norbert Balmer, whose wife hadn't attended, piloted Throcky skillfully through several tricky maneuvers.

He almost collided with Delfinnia and Phil Coffer who looked dead to the presence of anyone else. Dotson, he noticed, had backed a groggy Ford onto the dance floor with the expertise of a pro-driver putting an eighteen-wheeler through its paces.

"If you need any help parkin' that thing, let me know.' he told her.

At a tap on his shoulder he relinquished Alvina to the arms of her husband and had to dodge Colonel Pignut's bowed-leg antics as he headed off the floor.

Horace gave some consideration to joining his mother and Mr. Measles, but they were engrossed in what looked like a very serious discussion with Mrs. Snowberry. When all three looked in his direction, he knew it wasn't a place he wanted to visit.

As he reached the outskirts of the dance floor, he met Drusilla Sebastion with an underfed looking gentleman whom she introduced as "Alf" her husband. "I told you he'd come home when he got good and hungry," she said, with her roguish laugh.

As he watched these people who had become his good friends during the past year, he became aware that a piece of the puzzle was missing. Then it appeared.

Zack, who was still in his uniform, and Ladenia, who had changed in to a dazzling Christmasy looking green dress, sailed through the door and cruised onto the dance floor. She blew him a kiss accompanied by a wicked wink. It was obvious that the Navy's landing had been a success.

He stood alone and for the first time in many months he felt a deep pang of emptiness. As he turned away he caught sight of someone at the entrance to the dining room. It was Amanda. She was watching him with uncertainty.

As her wedding day had drawn close, she had taken a few weeks off from the office, but Horace had sent her a Christmas card with two tickets for her and her husband to attend the party as his special guests.

As he hurried toward her he thought she looked more like an angel than he remembered. Taking both her hands in his he said, "You got my invitation and I'm delighted you came. Now where is that new husband of yours?"

With the blush he'd always found so charming she said, "There isn't any husband. Over the last few months I'd begun to realize something very important was missing from our relationship and that was, that there was no true love. When I faced that, I knew I couldn't go through with it. It's all over including the tears, but I wanted to come by anyway, to thank you and wish you a Merry Christmas."

Taking her in his arms Horace said, "I'm so, sort of, terribly sorry."

She looked up at him, her eyes searching his face as she said, "Don't' be. I think I've found what I was missing".

With a rush of pure joy he spun her onto the dance floor. She stopped, and asked in surprise, "What's that big smile about?

"It's all about you and what just happened. It reminds me of an old Swedish proverb that I always felt was so true. *A life without love is like a year without summer."*

As he pulled her close, his glance fell on the huge window that overlooked the trees surrounding the clubhouse. The predicted snow had already started to fall and had turned the lighted landscape into a Christmas card he would cherish and remember for the rest of his life.

About the Author

I grew up in a wonderful happy family. A minister father and schoolteacher mother, four brothers and three sisters. After high school, I went to art school, which led me into interesting jobs all my life. For instance, in the Second World War, I joined the Navy Waves and was a mapmaker. From there, I branched into ad agencies, went on a trip to Hawaii, fell in love with it, and stayed for forty-two years. While there, I was involved with a design company, and we did many resorts as well as commercial offices.

When I returned to the mainland, although I retired (sort of), I kept busy in the graphic-art field and became interested in writing. I sold mainly short stories to church-related magazines. Then I wrote a book about a coworker who was dying of cancer. It was called "In the Shadow of Rainbows".

Writing Upson Downes—because of its humor and reaching out to accept, loving, and living with the human frailties we all have and still respecting each person—has been a joy.